Read and Enjoy

Alan Wright

# Catchers

Alan Winning-Wyatt

Published by

**MELROSE BOOKS**

An Imprint of Melrose Press Limited
St Thomas Place, Ely
Cambridgeshire
CB7 4GG, UK
www.melrosebooks.com


**FIRST EDITION**


Copyright © Alan Winning-Wyatt 2006

The Author asserts his moral right to
be identified as the author of this work


Cover and illustrations by *Maddie*

**ISBN 1 905226 67 5**

Printed and bound in Great Britain by:
CPI Bath, Lower Bristol Road,
Bath, BA2 3BL, UK

# Catchers

Legend has it that over 5,000 years ago man and Catchers lived and fought in harmony together, defending their civilisation against the destruction of themselves. Many stories were told and retold, many lives were affected, and many things learnt. This is the story of one such legend.

The bitter winter wind swept through the valley. High on the hills about were firs of every colour: from green and red through to yellow. A small stream flowed gently down the slope, breaking the land and feeding the main river that flowed off into the distance. Small villages nestled amongst the trees, their mud huts looking out of place with nature. Off in the distance a large stone frame covered the horizon, the walls of the great city Greatoak. On the hills caves sat foreboding and mysterious. The surrounding forests held creatures of various sizes and shapes. Some ate meat, others only vegetables. Fire-breathing dragons were among the meat eaters and caused the villages harm from time to time. One village, was made up of only a few mud huts and a dragon, had stumbled upon the odd scattered stick hut which, although small, was worth defending, so the men and Catchers thought. A Catcher was a small rodent like creature with a thick leathery skin of a burgundy colour, and thick dark spikes covered this. The Catcher was heavily built and had huge, strong shoulders. It was medium sized and had keen yellow eyes and moved as if part of the wind itself.

The dragon moved slowly and purposefully towards the camp, its nostrils already flared with the smell of fresh meat. Hungry, it had left the comfort of its lair in search of a fill, and having smelt its prey, the dragon had stumbled upon the village and now was embarking on having its meal then going back to savour its claim.

Stepping closer to the Catchers the dragon snarled and raised an angry paw. The Catchers scattered around its massive frame swinging their spiked tails at the hard scaly skin of the dragon; this had little if any effect at all. The men took a more direct approach and chose more cumbersome weapons such as swords, axes, and pikes. While the dragon advanced the men came in one fierce movement, catching the dragon directly under its eyelid. The dragon lurched in pain and the pike snapped, throwing the men to the ground and sending a huge ball of fire that engulfed the men and set alight the nearest huts. Devastation soon followed: huts were ablaze and bodies lay dead or dying in all directions in smouldering heaps.

While this was happening the Catchers had regrouped and were preparing for another attack. In one quick and accurate attack the Catchers moved upon the already distracted dragon. Climbing all over the main torso they began stabbing madly with their teeth and spikes, looking for vulnerable patches of skin. The dragon turned its attention towards the Catchers. This gave the men time to regroup and think again. The Catchers being the more formidable foe meant the dragon had to concentrate on them. The dragon drew up its huge torso and stood on its hind legs; swinging its tail it managed to sweep the Catchers from its body and spun them off in all directions. The Catchers were scattered only for a few seconds before they re-attacked the dragon. The dragon took a deep breath and sent a large ball of intense flame at the Catchers. Several were engulfed in the flame; however instead of harming the creatures they bathed in the flames by raising their spikes and allowing the energy to be absorbed into their bodies. Instantly these Catchers took the energy their bodies transformed, doubling in size and body weight, their whole body being made more muscular and streamlined. Full of vigour, the Catchers moved around the dragon continuing to distract it. The dragon now moved with an urgency and was throwing everything at the Catchers; each flame was caught and taken to use later as the Catchers grew stronger with each attack. The Catchers were now extremely large and dangerous looking creatures. Thanks to the distraction the men had regrouped and were back in the fight. Stabbing wildly at the fast moving dragon, one man caught the dragon with his pike. The dragon was furiously fighting several men and Catchers, taking blows. The Catchers moved as if one creature, working together as if controlled by thought. Quickly they backed away and concentrated the energy absorbed earlier. Sticking their tongues out, the Catchers sent raw energy at the dragon. Yellow heat covered its massive frame. Its body went rigid, then seemed to explode into thousands of pieces: each piece disintegrating as it flew in all directions. The dragon was gone and man and Catcher were safe once again.

Legend has it that the Catchers had found it necessary to create a force of energy to protect and heal man; this energy was to allow man to develop the land and live in harmony with the Catchers. The energy became known as 'the Source' and took on the form of a large honeycomb hanging from a large majestic oak in the centre on the city. However, to maintain the power needed constant care from the Catchers. The need to rekindle and care became ever increasing as man began to become ever greedier, taking not just what was necessary but more and more each time. As time went on man's greed got bigger and bigger, and man's acceptance of the Catchers less. Some time later, man began to suspect that the Catchers wanted the Source for themselves and began to force the Catchers away. Over the years the Source began to suffer and so did the Catchers. Eventually the Catchers ran to escape the inevitable and to survive as well as they could on their own. Leaving the safety and protection of the men, they fled to outer regions of the kingdom. Man had to learn to care for themselves and cope on their own. Man developed new skills quickly and survived with some good results.

A few hundred years had passed, and over the years the stories told of the Catchers had too. Eventually the stories became nothing but bedtime stories told to children, either to thrill or to put fear into the naughty ones. The fact that Catchers ever existed began to be questioned, and soon was virtually dismissed by all but a few. The Catchers soon became nothing but a legend themselves.

Elmstown was a quaint little village and was situated between two small hills on the edge of a secondary river running to the main coast. Its main employment was that of a fishing industry, and the folk living there lived well off the wide range of fish available. The folk – mainly human yet some leathery – had grown well accustomed to the river's funny ways, so had managed to create quite a market for themselves. Mainly stick houses, the village stood proudly in between the magnificent views cast by the hills. The village comprised a ship maker's, a village hall, a public house, a church, and a general store. Along with the houses, the village was of no interest to the surrounding villages other than for its fish: these were taken daily

by cart to the market at the city named Greatoak.

Greatoak was a vast complex of buildings that had stood the test of time for many years, in fact as far as memory allowed remembering. Within its walls stood many crafts, and along with these many folk of varying races. There were humans mainly, and also dwarves, elfin folk, leathery creatures, creatures that took on the form of twigs, and others. Along with these folk were people known as funny folk, aptly called this as they still practised the long forgotten and unneeded skills of swordsmanship and self-defence. These folk firmly believed that the time would come when these arts would be called upon again. They believed that the Source would one day relent, and then the city would once again be vulnerable to attack. One of these folk had moved into a small outbuilding on the edge of Elmstown. He was a quiet man, heavily built with muscles, and had a dark complexion due to outside activity. Kerstan Wholphsan was a man who kept himself to himself, training in the surrounding forests most of the day then returning to sleep. Over the year that he had been there he had become a recluse, forced to stay that way by rumours and fear, the only person daring to venture near his dwellings being the postal man if, on any odd occasion, a letter may have to be taken. In fact, all had heard of Kerstan in some shape or form, yet no one really knew anything about him, only the rumours they had heard. None had any idea where he had come from, or why he had ventured into their village in the first place.

Kerstan woke with a start; breathing heavily he fought to calm himself. What did the dream mean and why was it happening again? Only a candle lit the room, so Kerstan rolled out of bed and lit a lantern on the table. The cabin was small and cosy, within the cabin was his bed, a table, small cupboards made by his own hands, and a small sink. What did the dream mean? He had been in a dimly lit room along with several other folk, a wizard in a jade cloak holding a staff with a dark stone on the end, a large man who looked like he had the strength of an ox, an elf in magical clothing that blended in with the natural surroundings, and a small twig-like creature. They were studying what appeared to be a parchment, and had expected him? The wizard had spoken to him by name; it was at this point he always woke. Who was this wizard and how did he know him? What was the reason for the dream?

Kerstan rose and moved to the cupboard, within the cupboard was a bowl of fruit and one plate and bowl, both hand-carved from wood. Choosing an apple, he placed the bowl safely back and sat to eat it on the bed.

The cave shook and was filled with a thick mist of smoke smelling heavily of sulphur. Within its deep caverns was an angry creature screaming in frustration. Snode was a large creature that oozed evil: his arms were long and muscular yet covered in scars and mucus, his hands were strong with claws that glowed with a slight shimmer of red, his skin was a thick flaming ball of lava held together by some unseen material, and his long tail ended with three sharp spikes covered with dripping venom. His attention was focused on a timid looking leathery creature with large fear-filled eyes. The creature was trying to avoid eye contact with little success.

"How much longer must I wait? My magic is great and I have manipulated those worthless men causing devastation and jealousy among them, yet the Source still holds up and stops my entry into the city. It is mine – I shall have it."

The leathery creature shook violently throughout the onslaught yet stood its ground. Trying to speak, it failed through fear.

Snode turned his attention towards the fearful creature and sent an enormous ball of fire from deep within his arm which enveloped the creature. The creature was no more. Other creatures were now running and hiding trying to escape the frustration felt by Snode. One leathery creature spoke up bravely,

"We have created as many Sleepers as we can, it takes time to cre..."

Snode abruptly interrupted the creature with a ball of flame just over its head. The creature backed out quickly, leaving Snode alone with his thoughts once again.


The inn at Greatoak was filling up as usual; the happy buzz of conversation and the mixed races its usual intake. The bar was a grand affair, made of solid oak which had been hand crafted with fine elfin art, situated at the far end of a large hall full of hand-made oak tables with the same fine artwork. The room was lit with flaming torches, and hanging around the room was a variety of ornaments from the ancient war. A small dog slept happily in front of the open fire, which was burning nicely in the room. The Twisted Brier was a happy inn and was proudly owned by a couple of older elves. Alanthos was a friendly man who commanded authority and respect; he had fought in the past wars. His wife was a slight lady of beautiful qualities who had been a nurse in the wars. Her name was Slassiantha, and she had an unusual trait of seeming to float instead of walk: her whole demeanour angelic.

The wars had taken place a long time ago and had caused great loss between the men and the creatures that had fought. Many folk had lost family or knew of someone who had. All who had fought were respected for their courage and for defending the Source.

The inn's custom did not end with the drinking of their fine range of local and imported ales and beers; it was also the gathering place for various meetings. One such meeting was held regularly and in a private room above the kitchen where it was quiet. This meeting was attended by some of the funny folk.

In the room was a table that took up most of the space, and seated around the table were chairs, while two lanterns lit the room. The room took on a low-lit appearance and was occupied by several people. Spread out on the oak table was a large parchment. The parchment was being looked at by a man of around ten feet in height, his arms and legs at least the size of a tree trunk. In the corner of the room, watching him and supping on a fine ale, was an elf in clothing that seemed to change with every movement to blend in with the environment around him, and standing next to him, polishing a fine long bow and checking the flights of the arrows, was a small creature with a twig-like look. In the shadows was a man in a jade cloak with a staff, muttering an incantation to himself. As he did so the emerald on the tip of the staff was giving off a faint glow. The elf was the first to speak.

"Still trying that hocus pocus dream spell are you?" His voice was one of concern not ridicule.

The wizard opened his eyes and looked across at the elf. "Theorn, please be patient. It will take time but it is working, and if the rumours are right we will need Kerstan with us."

The elf replied quickly in an exasperated fashion. "How likely is it that one man took on a Sleeper and lived to talk about it yet alone beat it?"

"Believe just believe… We have to." The wizard replied as he re-shut his eyes to continue.


It was early in the morning and the air was fresh and cool. Kerstan had woken and after eating gone to take an early wake-up run. The dew hung heavy on the ground and every breath that Kerstan exhaled was a cloud of vapour. The same dream had woken him so he was clearing his head. While he made his way through the forest he mused over the dream – who were they and what did they want with him? He had travelled some distance when he came across a clearing in the wood and as he did his senses went mad: his hair pricked up on his neck and he sensed danger. Slowing, he approached with caution. Just before the clearing he stopped. The air had become eerie and damp, and he felt all his muscles tighten in anticipation, but what was the reason? He felt he had felt this feeling before as a child.

Upon reaching the clearing Kerstan gingerly looked around: although the area was now free of immediate danger, the scene was one of recent battle. Bushes were burnt or torn from their roots, the trees were missing branches, and some of the trunks were charred. Hanging precariously from one branch was the severely burnt body of a man who had been visibly shaken by something; two other bodies were backed in uncontrollable fear against a rock, both charred, one a young child with an arm missing. As Kerstan looked on in disbelief his first thoughts were to turn and leave, but he knew what had caused this devastation and felt anger for the helpless state of the victims. Only one creature was capable of this sort of attack, one from his past, yet why would anyone be foolish enough to re-create Sleepers from the ashes of a dragon? They had no master and were driven by an uncontrollable desire to destroy all, especially magical creatures.

His thoughts were interrupted by a strong sense of fear, and instantly he was aware of the intense feeling that he was not alone: the Sleeper had to be nearby. Moving into a defensive crouch, Kerstan surveyed the area. Everywhere he looked was normal looking, yet he could feel the fear. Sleepers used fear as an attack and used it effectively.

Rising slowly, Kerstan drew a small straight-bladed sword with a handle made from the leg bone of a boar. Keeping his wits and controlling his already wavering fear, Kerstan moved deeper back into the forest: the Sleeper had to be somewhere, it must have sensed his presence and returned. Kerstan was having to keep reminding himself to keep calm and was physically shaken as he controlled his breathing so as not to attract attention. As he moved to pass a tree he heard a noise and stopped to watch; a deer was moving into the area in search of food. Suddenly the deer looked up, pricking its ears up, and turned to run. As the deer ran, out of a thick area of trees came the Sleeper.

Although Kerstan had seen Sleepers before, he still felt the distaste in his throat. The Sleeper was a strange looking creature: its black skin was covered in oozing sores that were pussing with a slimy green thick liquid; its body was something like a wild cat's yet was larger; its legs resembled insects. The creature ran on four of its legs, and the other two had sharp claws which held a whip of an eerie purple flame and a large club which had rough sharp bits of bone jutting from it, together with a maggot-infested child's arm. The Sleeper's whole demeanour was one of a crazed creature totally bent on destruction.

The Sleeper was moving at a fierce pace and was gaining on the deer; Kerstan watched it leave and took a deep breath to try to calm himself. All his body ached from the last few minutes yet Kerstan forced himself to stand. He had to pursue the Sleeper; it was too close to the village and would return to kill again if not destroyed. Kerstan knew that the Sleeper was able to fight and destroy several opponents at a time, yet he had to go after it.

Gathering his fears, he made off in the direction the Sleeper had gone. The route was not hard to follow as the Sleeper had left a clear path of destruction: branches were snapped and bushes torn apart. The distance was quite a large one however, so Kerstan had to move quickly. As Kerstan raced to catch the Sleeper his mind was thinking over the situation: *Don't do this you are walking into a certain death, you're a fool, you have seen the damage before.*

His thoughts went back to his childhood and he saw his father and mother fighting to defend the village; he had been with them and had learnt to survive with them. His first experience of the Sleepers was when he was just five, Snode's parents had created the creatures to destroy the Catchers and man, and they had been created in anger and had caused great loss to the civilisation at the time. Kerstan's parents had been killed, and he had been adopted by the local witchdoctors and had grown up with their daughter. Snode's parents had died in the battle too, leaving him vulnerable, yet he had survived.

Kerstan forced himself to think of the present task. By now his fears were mounting and he needed to gather control over them again, he was approaching his target. Kerstan could hear in the distance a loud crunching of bones and flesh and was certain that the Sleeper was greedily feeding on its prey. Slowing, he crept to take a look.

At a short distance from him was the Sleeper, tearing menacingly on the deer's neck. Kerstan dropped to the floor instantly and waited for his chance to attack. The Sleeper stopped gnawing and started looking around, sensing movement nearby; fear was all around and ever increasing. The Sleeper drew itself up onto its legs and searched the area for the prey; lifting its whip it turned to look upon the crouching body of Kerstan. Slowly and deliberately the Sleeper moved closer towards Kerstan, its movement showing the confidence it felt of its certain victory. Kerstan saw that it was a young creature and steadied himself, readying for the attack.

As the Sleeper moved closer the whip sang through the air, only Kerstan's fast reactions meant that the flame missed him, setting a bush alight. The whip came again and as the whip was drawn back Kerstan somersaulted forwards, slicing a wide ark with his sword, but the Sleeper moved aside and Kerstan rolled heavily to his feet. Now the Sleeper moved again, this time using the club. Kerstan dived low and as he came back up lunged the sword once again in a low arch. Moving to avoid the blow, the creature was too slow. The tip sliced the underside of the Sleeper.

The Sleeper seemed surprised at the hit yet was soon back in the fight. Another blow from the club smashed heavily into Kerstan's leg, who had minimised the effect by rolling. However, the poison was in his bloodstream. Pain and nausea were already upon him, and Kerstan could feel himself drifting into a deep sleep. Fighting to keep himself awake, Kerstan moved to attack again. His sword was heavy but with skill he managed to hit the target and the Sleeper backed off again.

Kerstan was struggling to keep awake but knew to survive he had to. Putting his hand into his pocket, Kerstan drew out some grey powder. Turning once more he threw the powder at the Sleeper and rolled to his left towards an opening in the forest where the sun had broken through. The dust seemed to temporarily blind the creature and was causing some pain – the creature backed away again.

When the Sleeper recovered Kerstan was in the open. The creature, although angry, was unable to enter into the sun's rays. The Sleeper was in agony: its eyes felt as if acid was burning them, its skin had started to peel from its face and upper body, and as the puss was flowed freely, the Sleeper's discomfort increased. Kerstan dived once again at the Sleeper as it shielded its eyes from the light, and his actions were rewarded as the blade of the sword went deep before Kerstan pulled it free.

While the creature regained itself, Kerstan forced him to go on and made for the stream; he had to get to a broad-leafed plant that survived there. The plant was a dull orange and covered in hairs and had a rubbery texture. Known as mingalonion, the plant had been used before by Kerstan's relatives. Finding the plant, he ate it as quickly as he could. Vomiting violently, Kerstan felt better yet was

finding his vision was blurred; the Sleeper was still around so he had to concentrate.

The creature came again, its movement slow and uncertain and pain in its severely damaged face. But Kerstan was ready, and rolling plunged his sword deep into the Sleeper again. The Sleeper turned and was gone. Relaxing, Kerstan collapsed, breathing heavily as he munched on some more mingalonion plant.

The Sleeper had made its way slowly and confused. This was unexpected – there had been a man able to cope with the fear attack and cope well enough to fight back. This man had been so fast and skilled that his attacks had passed the Sleeper's defences, and what was that powder? It had caused extreme pain and on close inspection had made deep wounds that needed proper care, back at the lair. This man needed to be stopped, he needed to be reported and soon. The pain was so bad though, the need to rest was high and rest the Sleeper would. Once resting, the Sleeper found that its breathing was heavy and laboured, and then slowly it became thin, and a feeling of drifting came over the Sleeper, then warmth and finally peace. The Sleeper had run knowing that it was not able to fight as its vision was so bad. The Sleeper only travelled for a short distance before it collapsed and died by a tree. The body slowly returned to its original state of ash and steamed under the heat of the day.

After finishing the leaf and successfully emptying his stomach, did Kerstan know that the mingalonion had saved his life?


Snode had stirred in his sleep, something had awakened him and he now sensed the loss. He had lost control of a spirit under his control, but where and what he was not sure of. Settling down again Snode laid his heavy head on the floor once again sleep was heavy on his eyes. As he slept he dreamt of the destruction of Greatoak and the vengeance for his parents.


The room on the top floor of the Twisted Brier was empty other than for Slassiantha who was cleaning through, preparing the room for another meeting. The room was used daily by the same folk and always in secret, yet the pay was good so she had no real concerns, and she knew Xendon the wizard was a good man and a believer in the Source. As she worked dusting the fine table she whistled a merry tune to herself.

While she busied herself the inn was getting busy down below and the custom was good. Alanthos was his jovial self, telling stories of old and serving the various customers. The doors opened and in walked Xendon. After closing the door he acknowledged Alanthos, and indicated that he was going to the room. Alanthos smiled and nodded in reply. As he climbed the stairs the sound of Slassiantha whistling brought a smile to his face. Upon entering the room Xendon stood in the entrance for a few seconds watching her glide to and fro, busy and unaware of his presence. A short while later Slassiantha turned, and upon seeing Xendon a small scream left her mouth, but she soon recovered herself and smiled. Xendon quickly apologised for startling her then entered the room fully to place onto the table the parchment he was carrying. Slassiantha spoke quickly to break the silence.

"Have you any more news on the Sleepers?"

Xendon stiffened slightly at the mention of the Sleepers, then regained his composure quickly and unrolled the parchment.

"This is a map of the surrounding countries and marked on it are the various encounters so far with the time, date and results."

Xendon looked up briefly from the parchment before continuing,

"The last attack occurred yesterday just outside Elmstown on the outskirts of Berchtown, far too close to the city for my liking. However, this attack ended in an odd way, we found ash a few feet from the attack position and can only think the Sleeper died! How or when we have no idea – one explanation is that Kerstan lives near there so perhaps..."

Slassiantha abruptly interrupted at this point with a little excitement in her voice.

"Kerstan, I knew a Kerstan a long time ago, yet he vanished soon after the wars."

Xendon looked on as she spoke then went back to studying the parchment and allowed Slassiantha to make her excuses and leave. As she made to leave Theorn entered the room, talking to a small twig-like creature.

"That is interesting, Tinden," he said.

Xendon stopped his studying and turned to look towards Tinden and Theorn. Their manner was relaxed and showed a little excitement until they noticed that they were not alone.

"What is of interest then to both of you?"

Xendon spoke softly, smiling casually and looking both up and down squarely. The reaction was quick and full of both enthusiasm and excitement. Being from the race of Sprouters, Tinden should have been a shy creature. Sprouters were created from small plants by elf magic; most were excellent trackers at one with nature yet extremely timid. Tinden, however, was different – from a young twig he had craved attention. It was Tinden who spoke as he puffed out his chest proudly.

"We were down at the market looking when we spoke to Fragen, the dwarf that runs the weapons stall. He says that there is a man asking questions about us, his name was Kergan so he thought could this be Kerstan who we are looking for?"

Xendon looked from one of them to the other, a broad smile on his face. "There is only one way to find out for sure… So the dream spell may have worked." Xendon looked at Theorn as he spoke then returned to the parchment.

Leaving quickly, Tinden and Theorn made their way through the now busy inn, trying not to attract too much attention. Once outside they took the streets heading towards the market once again. Moving as quickly as they could, they entered the busy market and made their way to the weapons stall.

The market was a well-established affair, having been in operation for a very long time. The stalls were of various types and standards. They sold live products such as sheep and goats, armour, pottery, and the like, and in the market was a small and little-used stall that sold weapons. This stall was run by a small stocky dwarf, and in most people's eyes was an unnecessary stall as wars were far and few between since the Source had been created.

The market was well used by outsiders from all the surrounding towns and villages, so Theorn spoke in a guarded manner to Fragen who was as usual his over-friendly self. After talking, he was told that the man was last seen heading away from the market in an easterly direction, down the side streets towards the centre of the city. He had mentioned the chapel. Theorn thanked Fragen then turned and made his way back to Xendon to tell of his findings. Once back in the upper room he aired his fears to Xendon.

"If this man is Kerstan then he is one of the only survivors of the Last War from the tribes of old. He is also rumoured to be highly magical and the only man to fight and destroy Sleepers single handed. If this is true why bring his type back here?"

Xendon gave a large sigh before answering his friend. When he did it was a firm and rapid response.

"We will need his skill and knowledge of battle if my theories are correct."

After listening, Theorn gave Xendon a reassuring smile and shrugged his shoulders, then waited to see the next move.

14

Having taken a good look around the market, Kerstan had spoken as carefully as he could to the stall holders to find any information on the people in his dream. But not having much luck, he had decided to go to the chapel: there he would hopefully find the answers he was after, as most folk who fought in wars believed in something and therefore went to the place where that something resided.

Like most cities, Greatoak placed the chapel towards the centre in the city's defences because of its importance. The chapel was a grand affair, built by elves with great affection, and intricate elfish runes were carved into the vast frame, which towered high on the horizon for the city folk to look upon. Inside, the walls had delicate carvings and statues depicting stories of old involving man and Catchers as they lived and fought in harmony. The whole building had been constructed around the great oak itself: this oak had the Source growing on its mighty frame and stood a few hundred feet high in the inner chamber, hidden from view and harm.

The Source was protected by a magical race left to tend for it by the Catchers who had fled a long time ago. It was so hidden that most city folk knew little if anything of its presence. The Zenithe had decided it best that the Source stayed hidden and that was how it had been for years. Zenithe were very tall, sometimes reaching nearly fifteen feet, and their appearance was that of a human yet they were of angelic properties. Highly magical and deeply religious, the Zenithe lived to protect the Source and were a peaceful race on the whole. Their movement was smooth and effortless and gave a calming feeling to those that saw them.

Kerstan had made his way slowly towards the chapel, watching his surroundings carefully, hoping to pick up any clues to the whereabouts of the folk in his dream. Arriving at the chapel no better off than when he had left the market, he entered through the great oak doors quietly. Once inside, Kerstan looked around the building with some interest at the carvings and statues before kneeling to pay his respects to his God. All around the Zenithe continued to clean and dust the interior. Some Zenithe who were facing a statue of two Catchers nursing the Source, started to quietly sing, an angelic song that filled the room with a strong presence of great peace and made Kerstan feel a little light-headed. Having paid his respects, he rose and slowly looked around once again, waiting for the opportunity to speak to one of the Zenithe. A short while passed until Kerstan was approached by one of the Zenithe. Upon reaching him, the Zenithe gently placed one of his unusually long arms onto Kerstan's shoulder. Kerstan felt a strong feeling of warmth then heard an echoing voice that floated into his head, although the Zenithe had not opened his mouth.

"Welcome, stranger, to the chapel of rest. Feel free to spend as long as you need."

The Zenithe's eyes bore deep into Kerstan, not in a menacing way but with concern and love. The Zenithe did not move his arm yet continued to pour his love and power onto Kerstan.

"If you are who you say you are, you may. But you must be quick and show respect."

The Zenithe had spoken again; the words confused Kerstan yet he was being gently guided by the Zenithe towards a door in the centre of the chamber. Once they had reached the door, the Zenithe spoke some words and the door gently opened. Once inside the door, the bright light took Kerstan a few seconds to adjust to, then once his vision returned before him was an incredible sight.

There before him was a massive and mighty oak. Its great trunk was rooted deep into the ground and it had draped all over its mighty branches a glowing honeycomb skin. The skin seemed to be glowing dimmer and brighter in a rhythmic fashion as if breathing, and around the skin were several more Zenithe that were older than the one that had spoken to Kerstan. The feeling of immense power was everywhere and the Zenithe seemed to be busy tending to the honeycomb. The Zenithe at no time touched the Source, and at no time stopped to acknowledge Kerstan. Kerstan just stood still, trying to take in the scene before him. His whole body ached with the power that was everywhere. Suddenly he felt a deep feeling inside his head and sensed that the Source was about to speak; in a delicate feminine voice it spoke.

"Friend of Catchers, you are welcome."

Kerstan felt a mix of emotions: he felt confused, angry and unsure all at the same time.

"Why do you fear? Move closer, touch, and I will teach you."

Kerstan hesitated, then felt the urge to reach out to touch the honeycomb. As he did the young Zenithe made to stop him. The Zenithe suddenly stopped and seemed to be full of remorse before backing away and leaving the chamber bowing low. Kerstan continued to move towards the Source and gently touched the surface. Instantly his whole body felt as if it was in flames; tremendous power flowed all over him and his mind was filled with visions of the past and some possibly of the future.

Kerstan could only stand for a few seconds before he collapsed, feeling drained and confused. The visions were filling his mind, mixing and confusing. He felt sick and weak, yet at tremendous peace with himself. The Source seemed to be drained of colour as Kerstan staggered to his feet once again. The young Zenithe returned and ushered Kerstan back into the outer chamber then, after shutting the door, returned to working. Once Kerstan recovered all he wanted to do was leave the chapel as quickly as he could; he did not know why but felt he had to all the same. Kerstan rose and left, beginning his search for the folk once again. Upon leaving the chapel he made his way to the inn, as most folk went there and the likelihood was that someone would have information on the folk he wanted.

The man had been whistling cheerfully to himself, glad that he had managed to catch a good amount of fish. He had boxed them, then filled the cart, and had travelled early to make the start of the market. This he did weekly and with some success, managing to keep his wife and child fairly happy on the money he gathered. He had travelled most of the way along the route from Elmstown to the city when he had felt the presence. Great fear had fallen on him and he had tried to seek out the reason. It had happened quickly when the form had left its place in the shadows, a foul looking creature. The Sleeper was quick and deadly, and had attacked, needing to help its craving for death. The man had tried to fight yet fear had beaten him, and he had not lasted long the Sleeper had torn him to pieces and then devoured his main body and lower limbs before moving on again.

Xendon, Theorn and Tinden talked over the action they should take next. Once a decision had been made, they tidied their various belongings and made for the main floor of the inn. Entering, Theorn made his way over to the bar and spoke briefly with Alanthos before handing over the payment due for the room. The inn, although filling nicely with a variety of folk, took little notice of their actions. Turning, the group made to leave, but as they headed for the door it opened and in walked Kerstan. Unsure what action to take, Xendon (who recognised him through his dreams) hesitated. Theorn and Tinden waited awkwardly as well, unsure of Xendon.

Upon entering, Kerstan took a couple of seconds to adjust his eyes, then saw standing before him the robed man in his dream. Instinctively, he drew his sword a little before replacing it firmly in his scabbard. Kerstan quickly scanned the inn and recognised two other folk also, slowly he made his way into the inn and approached the bar, keeping an eye on Xendon. Having bought a drink, he stood at the bar and waited to see what they would do. Xendon sat at a nearby table followed slowly by Theorn and Tinden, who by now were both aware of Kerstan however uncertain of who he was. Xendon spoke quietly under his breath to explain, then decided it was best to return to the room above along with the others, in the hope that Kerstan may just follow. As they rose and headed for the rear door the main door opened, and in walked Shadma with a large sack of barley over his shoulder. He stopped in the doorway, uncertain of what to do, then decided to put the sack dawn on the bar as first intended.

"Here is your barley as promised, Alanthos. Should feed your ox for a while."

As he spoke he was watching the movement of the others, sensing something was not normal. He took a seat and waited, watching them move upstairs shortly followed by a ranger. Once they had left he slowly followed from a distance.

Xendon quickly took a seat, placing it facing the door, and sat down trying to look calm. Theorn and Tinden stood a distance from him and watched the door also. Listening, they heard the stairs being taken cautiously, then they heard a cry and some sort of struggle. Waiting and unsure of their next move, they listened. Suddenly, Shadma fell through the door onto the floor, followed by a very angry ranger.

"Try an ambush would you? I suggest you talk and fast. Make it good."

Shadma looked totally shocked at the ease that he had been beaten, but slowly raised himself to his feet. Xendon spoke quickly.

"No ambush was meant, we need to speak to you on a matter of some urgency."

Xendon gestured that Kerstan enter the room properly and take a seat. Kerstan entered a little but no seat was taken. Watching them closely, he gestured that Xendon speak more. Xendon took a deep breath and slowly tried to explain all he knew of the attacks made by the Sleepers, and of his theories of an impending attack from an unknown creature at present. He also asked that Kerstan join them in trying to defend the city. Kerstan listened carefully to the conversation, which had taken most of several hours, then spoke in a calmer manner.

"My theory is that this whole issue with the Sleepers has something to do with the Source, as they only normally attack magical things."

Kerstan let his statement hit the listeners before continuing.

"I see you believe in the Source. Rightly so, as I have spoken to the Source just recently. She seems to think the same and has asked for my help also."

Conversation went on deep into the evening, and finally it was settled that they would all meet to discuss things further the next day. Kerstan rose and before leaving turned to speak one more time.

"The Source spoke of the need for help from the Catchers."

His voice was one of controlled uncertainty.

"I believe they still exist, as I have felt their presence before when out training."

Leaving these thoughts with the folk he turned to leave, then thought again.

"I will try to teach you what I know of the Sleepers, their weaknesses – the few there are – and hopefully methods of defeating them."

Then he was gone, leaving Xendon, Theorn, Tinden and Shadma to talk some more.

Once outside the room, Kerstan walked slowly back down the stairs. Upon entering the inn, he found it lit softly by one lantern and the open fire. Alanthos was sitting having a quiet drink with three other folk. Looking up, Alanthos asked if all was alright, then happily returned to his drink. Kerstan left the inn and the conversation, and made his way through the now cold crisp air towards the river, where he had left a raft to take him back to Elmstown. Passing homes now lit and full of families oblivious to the day's conversation, he walked slowly. Taking in every detail and he thought how all this could change if Xendon was right. The night seemed so perfect: the night creatures were coming out, the lamps in the homes dimly glowing, and the sound of the nearby river was soothing, as it rolled peacefully by on its route to the sea. It took several minutes to reach the edge of the river where he began searching the bank for where he had tied his raft. Upon finding it he paused to stare out across the river, before going to step onto the raft. It was at this point he heard the sound of movement behind him. Turning and drawing his sword in one quick smooth move, he came face to face with Slassiantha. Startled by the move, she glided back a little way,

"How did you get so close without me hearing you?" Kerstan spoke in a stern voice.

Slassiantha smiled and floated closer slowly. "Hello, Kerstan. It has been a while. I am Slassiantha."

Kerstan stood and looked her up and down before answering.

"My you have grown, yet it can't be you as you were taken by trolls when you were just five."

Slassiantha answered quietly with a trembling voice.

"I was young yet I survived thanks to your parents." There was a bitter tone in her voice as she spoke.

Stepping onto the raft he turned and spoke as he pushed off.

"Be proud of your parents. I was, as they were of you right to the end."

Slassiantha stood and watched the raft drift away before turning to return to the inn, thinking upon her conversation with Kerstan. When she arrived back she continued to tidy without a word. Alanthos noticed, but knew well enough to wait for answers.

Kerstan had known Slassiantha and her parents from a young age; he had grown up in the village and learnt their skills. As witch doctors and well respected, they had taught magic to Slassiantha and him at a young age. They had been pleased with the way they had learnt, although they had commented that Slassiantha had a special power, the nature of which they had not said. However, at a young age he had become ill and they had given him a blood transfusion: saved his life but then been thrown out of the camp, banished. He had never known why and had been too young to ask. His parents had taken in Slassiantha until war took them away and the trolls that killed them took Slassiantha as well. He had searched her parents out and nursed them through the hard times all the way to their death, never once had they talked of their banishment and never had he dared to ask. They had often asked of their daughter and he had hidden the truth from them, telling that she was fine, considering it easier to keep the wars and the capture from them.

It did not take long to travel along the river back to Elmstown, and Kerstan was soon in the security of his home. Lighting a fire, he sat to eat a few scraps that he had in the cupboard. After eating, he settled down to sleep and thought of Slassiantha once more. Should he tell her about her parents or was it better to keep quiet? He would have to consider.

Early the next morning, Kerstan set off back for the raft, then swiftly steered back to the city and tied up to a post just off the bank. The air was crisp and an early mist was still present. Having successfully tied the boat, he made his way back to the inn. Knocking at the door he waited, and shortly Alanthos opened the door a crack then popped his head out.

"Come in, Xendon has arrived, he informed me of the meeting last night." Alanthos quickly ushered him in then shut the door, re-locking it. Waiting in the room and sitting near the newly lit fire were Xendon and Shadma. Talking could be heard from the kitchen just off the bar, and it was not long before Slassiantha, Theorn and Tinden were coming in holding fresh bread, warm from the stove. They all sat around a small table that had been brought in from the scullery, and the parchment was placed out flat upon it ready to study.

"Here is a map of the surrounding area. It has become apparent that Sleepers have been re-created by someone of incredible magic. The only reason we can assume is to destroy something magic."

Xendon was speaking in hushed tones as the inn was not officially open and he did not want to draw attention.

"Kerstan has been to see the Source. The Source has indicated that what we have assumed for a while could be correct, Kerstan."

Turning to Kerstan who sat up abruptly at the mention of his name, Xendon indicated that he should continue to speak.

"I was privileged to speak to the Source, and She has said that she has felt a drain on her for years from an outside cause. She needs to get help. She is not well."

Several murmurs echoed around as he spoke.

"It has been mentioned that Catchers may help, one in particular, by the name of Zandibar."

The conversation soon took on a more intense fashion, lasting until Alanthos spoke.

"Sorry. I am going to have to open the inn."

Kerstan answered him quickly. "I will go in search of the Catchers. I'll leave early tomorrow and I will be taking a tracker with me called Mutley. He will find the Catchers if they are still alive."

Standing before anyone could stop him, he turned to leave. Then he spoke once more. "I hope that the methods I have spoken about for fighting Sleepers will be of help. Most importantly though, remember to control your fear."

Alanthos opened the door, and silently and quickly the group left back into the streets covered by the early mist.


Snode slept soundly in his cave. The room echoed with his snores.

As he slept, deep in the mass of caves several leathery creatures were working hard creating Sleepers from dragon ash. Each Sleeper was created in a special cave covered in a deep evil magic which encompassed them so that they could not attack, then when needed they were released through a back exit to do their master's bidding.

News had arrived at the caves from a small creature that looked like a monkey but had huge eyes for seeing clearly in the night. The news was not good, and had to be taken to Snode. The leathery creature in charge took a deep breath and, trembling, made his way up the passages to the sleeping quarters of Snode.

"Gracious Lord, I have news of some urgency."

Snode shifted awkwardly before opening one eye lazily.

"What is important enough to wake me?" he muttered.

The commander squirmed, took a deep breath then spoke.

"It has been reported that some Sleeper ash was found near a small village. A man was captured and tortured, and has reported that a ranger had killed it, so it was rumoured."

"WHAT!" bellowed Snode. "Who is this man?"

The commander was getting more nervous as the conversation continued and was squirming badly. "I don't know. The man died soon after telling us what we know."

Snode turned a funny shade of red then seemed to visibly calm.

"Send out trolls to find this man who dares to kill my creation, and kill him and bring his head to me."

The commander bowed low and backed out, thankful that he had survived the meeting. Snode rubbed his rough hand over his face and shrugged off the feeling of sleep, then started making plans to attack the city.

Theorn had made a choice to go to his birth land to gather help from his cousin and his kind – he was sure that they would help. Having set off, he found that the journey was taking too long. He had to travel through shrub land to get to his birth land and it was hard work, and he found himself becoming frustrated with how the day was turning out. He had only been travelling for around two hours when darkness began covering the land; having spent most of his youth out in the open as a ranger this was not a problem to him. Looking around, Theorn chose a nice spot a few hundred yards away next to some rocks; it would give him natural shelter. The smoke that was coming off the fire was thick, and Theorn was concerned that it may attract an unwanted predator to his whereabouts; but the fire soon took well with the smoke subsiding so all was well. The light was barely enough to see a few feet away, so Theorn began to relax and pulled out his bedding from his pack, laying it out to sleep.

He had only slept a short while when he was awoken by a noise. Rolling onto his elbows Theorn studied the direction of the noise;

the fire was of no help as it had gone out, leaving just smouldering embers. Lying still and concentrating on the direction of the noise, Theorn could soon make out shadowy figures heading in his direction; they would pass by a short distance from him. One of the figures was carrying a torch that flickered in the wind, giving off just enough light to show the occupant was an orc. Its small wiry body had extremely ugly features and it was talking to another orc. Theorn lay quietly to determine the number of orcs and their intentions. Why would orcs be travelling in numbers in the dead of night? Sinking lower in the grass he waited for them to pass. There were around fifty of them, lightly armoured but carrying a variety of weapons. Theorn could now hear the nearest talking in a low whisper.

"Why is it that us orcs always have the dirty work to do?"

The other orc grunted in approval as the first went on. "Attack the surrounding villages, He said, then wait for the main army."

The other orc spoke up with an agitated attitude. "Yeah, as if we can't take a city by night when unexpected."

Conversation was getting harder to hear as the orcs moved on. Theorn waited a little longer thinking fast of what to do. The orcs were moving on into the distance so Theorn waited for the party to distance themselves, hoping for some slower orcs that may have separated themselves from the main party. It wasn't long before Theorn's wait was rewarded: two younger orcs were a short distance behind and one seemed to be limping. Both moaned about the distance travelled and the lack of comfort. Theorn rose silently and stayed in the shadows; with quick accuracy he fired off a deadly arrow at the injured orc who took the arrow through the back of the head, dropping quietly. The second was not certain if his friend had stumbled or been shot, so hesitated to find out. Theorn moved on the orc like a hungry lion, knocking the orc clean off his feet. Theorn held the orc's mouth tightly as he fell, to prevent him alerting the others. Theorn had a weight advantage and, after a short tussle, had the youngster held firmly to the ground. Hissing angrily in the orc's ear he spoke…

"What army are you waiting for, who is in command? Tell me or die."

The young orc was shaking visibly and breathing hard, yet he fought to escape and refused to speak.

"Tell me!" he snarled. "Last chance," taunted Theorn.

Loosening his grip, he allowed the orc to breathe easier, but the orc was quick to react and struggled free of his arm. Theorn took a nasty blow to the cheek and let go of his foe. The orc was struggling to his feet and Theorn threw himself hard onto the orc once again. A load crack was heard and the orc lay silent, his head at a funny angle. Theorn punched the ground in anger before rising once again.

Quickening his pace in the opposite direction of the orcs, Theorn made towards his homeland by the cover of darkness, the urgency was more now than when he had first left. Travelling at a great speed he covered the distance, and was soon nearing the sycamore stream; although its currents were fast and sometimes treacherous he did not hesitate crossing wildly to the other side. His journey's end was not that far now and he could make out the tall trees that surrounded his old village.

Theorn slowed as his eyes adjusted to the light. Above the trees Theorn could make out thick smoke, and it seemed to be coming from where the village was. His heart quickening, Theorn turned to his right and made his way around the trees to look at the village from above. Once through the trees and into the clearing Theorn could see the reason for the smoke. The village lay in complete carnage: huts were aflame, fencing smashed with the cattle running wildly around. Village folk lay dead, scattered around the camp. Someone had been there recently and attacked by night, taking his fellow elves by surprise. He had been too late to give the warning.

Sitting heavily, Theorn gazed at the vision of disaster, his heart heavy from both the journey and the outcome. Turning suddenly, Theorn heard a crack and went for his bow. An arrow landed close to his body and a voice warned him to stay still, then three elves dropped from the trees. The nearest took Theorn and bound his arms, then roughly guided him down the bank and deeper into the woods.

Once through the trees, Theorn could make out a small, quickly assembled camp with around twenty elves all tired and battle scarred. Theorn was pushed hard towards the leader and stumbled to the floor, landing hard on his face, unable to stop the impact. The leader studied him then gestured that his ropes should be untied and he should be allowed to speak. Rubbing his wrists and face, Theorn sat on the floor and studied his kinfolk, who looked at him with suspicion, waiting for him to speak. Theorn chose his words carefully and tried to keep to the facts. He spoke of the meetings that he had spent with Xendon, Tinden and Shadma, of when Kerstan arrived and of their findings, then of his recent encounter with the orcs. After speaking, he asked the villagers what had occurred recently. The same orc party had attacked their camp by surprise, and although they had fought hard and well, killing at least half the orcs, they had lost most of the village folk. Theorn listened intently, then asked after his cousin and was informed that he had been killed defending his daughter and wife. It was decided that the need to go and defend the city was more than to try to rebuild the village.

"We will need to split ourselves into groups to gather as much backup help to defend the Source back at Greatoak. Something sinister is planning to destroy us all."

"So the Source is real! Tell us more."

Theorn sat and told all he knew, then the groups split up into two smaller groups. One was just five lead by Shant and Henthal, both great fighters and able to take control. The rest would make their way back to Greatoak to see what help they could be, taking a small detour to attack the orc party that was heading to the outskirt village to wait.

Theorn and Manathorin, the leader, took an cautious route to Dewtown, the small village that the orcs had headed for when Theorn had seen them last. The light was just returning so an attack could be a little hard to do by surprise. The party slowed and waited on a brow of a hill that had a reasonable view of the small, recently attacked village. Villagers were being guarded and taken prisoner, and the orcs had temporarily repaired the gates and were making themselves at home ready for the long wait ahead. Theorn glanced across at Manathorin, who was talking in hushed tones to his troops and gesturing in the direction of the village. The four he had spoken to made off, taking a long route avoiding the open spaces to get to a small clump of trees near the back of the village. Others were checking their arrows and weapons and looking a mixture of anxious and angry. Manathorin turned to Theorn and smiled.

"Good to be back in a battle where we have the upper hand," he said.

As he spoke two elves clothed in grey cloth made their way from his side, carefully avoiding the gaze of the village, which was not too hard as the orcs were busying themselves with other things. Once close enough they scaled the wall with ease, using the overgrown foliage that was attached to the wall. Once up they quickly went over and disappeared from view.

Meanwhile, as this happened one of the four that had left was distracting the orcs by a fine display of being drunk as he made his way through the back gate and into the village. Once inside, upon seeing the orcs he ran back out and headed for the trees where the others were hiding. This managed to draw a few orcs in pursuit, then once near enough to the wood archers attacked them from the trees. The two inside were releasing the prisoners after successfully killing the guard, and then making their way to help to open the main gate. Meanwhile as confusion ruled, Manathorin, Theorn, and the rest charged the main gate to try to break it down. The orcs were caught off guard and suffered great loss, and after a short battle from all sides they lost the fight. Dewtown was safe once again.

Snode's army was growing daily and its huge size slowly made its way along in a straight path for Greatoak, destroying as it went. Trolls, ogres, and the like, had joined the ranks and many villages and towns had suffered loss or total destruction. Roseville, a small village, had suffered particularly badly: the villagers had seen the army coming yet had not been prepared or trained for battle, and although they tried to resist loss was great and the village destroyed. Thistleville had been better prepared and had held off the vast army for several days, taking with their destruction a good number of the enemy, however the army was still advancing slowly on Greatoak and it would only be a while longer before Greatoak needed to fight itself.

Thistleville had seen them coming and sent a warning to other neighbouring towns and villages in the form of horsemen. Closing the perimeter gates they had prepared to fight. There were thousands of orcs heading slowly to take the village yet the troops, led by Blandithorpe, a mature fighter of years of battle history, had stayed in control through bravery and trust in their leader. Flaming arrows and burning cauldrons were sent at the orcs; this slowed them but only temporarily as the numbers were so vast. Under Blandithorpe's command the gates had held for three days, but then the inevitable happened and the gates had given way. Once it was clear that the battle was lost, Blandithorpe had taken his last of the troops and headed for Greatoak and safety.

It was early in the morning when the sun's rays crept over the misty horizon that the knock had come at Kerstan's door. Xendon, Tinden, and Shadma waited for an answer, then not getting one knocked again louder.

"Surely he has not left already? We needed to help by going with him."

Tinden spoke in an agitated manner, watching the vapour rise from his mouth as he did. Kerstan appeared from the woods nearby and with him was a strange looking man; his hair was long and his features were wiry and thin yet muscular and nimble all the same. He wore animal skins and moved with a deep interest in the surroundings, constantly bending, checking, and smelling the air. His whole demeanour was one of fear, and he fidgeted constantly. Upon seeing them, Kerstan took hold of the startled man and introduced him.

"This man is Mutley and he is a tracker, a fine one at that."

Kerstan smiled at the men then continued. "The last place to see a Catcher was Kalantrouther, the other side of the Black Mountains, and that was several months ago."

Shadma was quick to respond. "That is at least a week's journey away and time is short."

Kerstan stood his ground and spoke with authority. "It has been done in two days by Mutley."

He glanced at Mutley as he spoke. "The journey was not good and meant travelling through the Black Mountains and Zinobian country."

Xendon shook his head as his frustration started to show.

"We haven't the time to argue or risk taking such a stupid route, Zinobians will never let you through even if you could pass through the mountains."

Kerstan looked sombre and shrugged his shoulders. "We have no choice, so I go alone with Mutley to find the Catchers."

Tinden spoke in a confident manner, raising his voice to be heard. "I'll go with you. I'm good in the country."

Kerstan went to argue as into the clearing walked Alanthos and Slassiantha. Slassiantha spoke in a quiet manner.

"I think I should go with you. It makes sense." She smiled awkwardly then continued. "I am a woman so I may just live long enough to talk."

Reluctant as he was to do so, Kerstan had to agree; ignoring the others he indicated that he would accept her company.

Mutley was showing signs of wanting to get inside, away from any predators that might be watching, so they all made their way into Kerstan's home. The space was limited so everyone spoke quickly so that they could leave once again.

"I will stay for one more day and teach what I can of techniques on beating Sleepers, then we must leave."

After the conversation, all had agreed that Slassiantha was to go.

Tinden would find another way to help instead.

Early the next day Kerstan began showing the city folk the skills he had learnt, then, allowing them to try them, would correct and re-train until he was a little happier with the results. The day was drawing to the evening, so Kerstan recapped the basics.

"Remember, control your fear at all times, keep your movement varied – they hate that – swipe not stab, and twist the blade upon contact. Most importantly though…"

Kerstan had raised his voice as he was emphasising his words loudly.

"YOU MUST CONTROL YOUR FEAR AT ALL TIMES."

Tinden and Shadma were to leave to try to get help from Shadma's kind, a hard thing to do as giants were solitary creatures and distrusted humans. Xendon and Alanthos would stay in the city and keep training and re-training the folk as they arrived. Theorn had arrived with seven elves, all tired from recent battle yet glad to be at the city. After getting the village folk settled, Blandithorpe had left to search for more help once again. Repairs were being undertaken of the walls and the main area for potential attack. Upon returning he reported that no orcs had been seen for at least three days of the journey.

Kerstan and Slassiantha decided that the time to leave for the Black Mountains had come so they left along with Mutley, heading south-easterly to avoid being seen leaving. It was early morning when they set off at a reasonable pace, trying to keep Mutley moving and occupied so as not to allow for panic. Mutley seemed happy to be on the move again and soon was at home in the wilderness. Slassiantha spent the first part of the journey in quiet. The party had travelled for around twenty minutes and not met anyone, and Kerstan was looking around a little anxiously.

"Where is everyone?"

He spoke more to himself than to the rest of the party however Mutley replied curtly.

"All in hiding, I'd presume. There's quite a tense feeling around."

Slassiantha was keeping up with the group with little difficulty and was showing no signs of tiring. In the distance was the distinct bleak outline of the Black Mountains, sheer mountains of slate that always brought a strong feeling of fear and boding. Awesome as they looked, very few who entered left to tell the tale; the mountainside had a tendency to collapse, taking vast areas out at a time. Vegetation was scarce and the road through treacherous, inhabited by creatures known as Clickers that hunted to live, good at their living as well. They were known as Clickers as that was the noise they made when moving fast to attack, often the last noise heard by anyone. Half human, half lizard with thick black scaly skin and a thick armour on their back, they clung with suckers to the slate and stared out with their glowing yellow eyes in wait for their next meal. Water was so far and few between that to enter without a supply, or the skill to find it, would be foolish and the walls of the Black Mountains were so high they seemed to extinguish the light from the area. Mist would accompany wherever you trod and the air smelt of death. Most folk would decide to take the long route and go around the mountains, adding around a week to the journey but arriving in one piece.

"Are you sure we need to go through there?" Slassiantha spoke, her eyes locked in horror at the vision before her.

Kerstan looked across and back at her, then smiled before the same fixed gaze returned to his face.

"We need to find the Catchers if they still exist, before it is too late."

Mutley dropped to the ground and all went silent. His keen eyes scanned the horizon and he smelt the ground that he had pinched, rubbing it gently between his skilled hands. Then, just as quickly, he stopped. He rose and continued towards the mountains once again, no word having been spoken. The mist was beginning to encircle the small party and visibility was beginning to diminish due to the foreboding outline before them. Already the atmosphere was a tense one, the smell of death reaching the noses of the party. Vegetation was becoming scarce and upon scrutiny so was the animal population.

"We're near the Devil's Entrance."

Mutley's queer voice broke the silence, causing the party to slow and regroup before continuing. The Devil's Entrance was aptly named, as it was the only way into the Black Mountains and narrowed considerably so was an easy place for ambush. Mutley was showing signs of agitation: his eyes were in every direction, his body tense and ready to take flight if necessary. He stopped frequently, dropping and testing his surroundings before moving on. The mist was all around now and the light had severely diminished so that the party felt it was early evening. With visibility dropping constantly, the party slowed to a slow pace, keeping in a tight formation. It was Kerstan who saw the Clickers first, stuck to a wall ahead of the party. The Clickers watched the party approach. Three in all, their keen eyes picking up the party long before being seen themselves.

Their dark black bodies had a camouflaging effect and their only real visible feature was their yellow eyes.

Kerstan drew his sword. This caused the others to follow in drawing their weapons too; Slassiantha had a short sword with an arrangement of sharp edges coming from its base, delicately protecting the handle. Mutley had a sling and some fine smooth stones. It was not long before the whole party saw them, two others had joined the small welcoming party and the Clickers were moving swiftly down the sheer walls at a quick pace, their nimble bodies accustomed to the surface, their speed and movement swift and easy. Kerstan moved at an incredible pace, covering the ground between the Clickers and the party, his highly skilled movements allowing him to attack before the Clickers. Cutting deep with one swift slice, Kerstan killed one Clicker; its head hit the floor before its body. However, the others were all over him and tearing with their razor sharp teeth and claws. Only his highly trained body and unnatural speed allowed Kerstan to remain on his feet unscathed.


Slassiantha had joined the fight and was swinging blows into the fray, knocking the creatures off only for them to return. Mutley fired accurate stones at the foe, hitting them and causing minor injuries and slowing their movements. Kerstan rolled to the ground then back to his feet, and in doing so released himself from the clasp of one of the Clickers. The Clickers were happy in the environment and moved in and out of the mist with ease, creating gaps in the attack to their advantage. Kerstan cut another deeply with his blade, and with agility beyond a normal man avoided several attacks before he took a bite to the shoulder from another. Slassiantha, finding the opportunity to hit the Clicker as it attached itself to Kerstan (the other times Clickers moved too quickly, matching blow with counter blow and avoiding her efforts), finished the Clicker's attack by stabbing through with her blade, making use of the handle at every opportunity. Stones were flying in at a quick pace, helping in distracting the creatures. With two left and one injured badly, the Clickers turned and left, their stench staying for a while, caught in the mist. Each member stood scanning for the Clickers, reassuring the departure before regrouping.

Kerstan winced as he moved towards Slassiantha. Upon investigation the damage to his shoulder was deep and the tissue smelt of venom. Slassiantha took her backpack off and searched its contents for her supply of water, pouring half over the wound to flush the venom free from the open flesh. Taking some cloth she then bound the wound tightly with Kerstan trying to discourage her, so she apologised as she did. Mutley scanned the area all the time, his keen eyes taking in all around.

"Keep a close eye on that, the saliva is foul and may fester."

Mutley spoke quietly before starting off again, not to encourage a repeat of the last attack.

Moving carefully, Mutley made his way through the small gap and into the start of the Black Mountains followed by Kerstan and Slassiantha. The ambush was unsuccessful and the party moved on. The road narrowed considerably and all was dark. The way ahead would be treacherous.

"How did you move so swiftly? You were able to hit them, even avoid their attacks." Mutley spoke out in amazement breaking the awkward silence. "I have never seen Clickers beaten before."

Kerstan looked across at Mutley but chose to stay silent as he walked on, keeping a watchful eye on the mist and darkness before him. Slowly Mutley led the party deeper into the mist and further into the centre of the Black Mountains.

The city was filling with busy, anxious people, the walls and gates had been given some long overdue repairs and the battlements were being filled with large vessels holding oil for defensive action against enemy attack. Alanthos had busied himself in training the new arrivals after Xendon sent them to get armour and weapons from the city armoury. Xendon had also visited the chapel to see the Zenithe and to check on the condition of the Source. Theorn had returned in the late afternoon along with a small army of elves, well armoured and trained. The elves soon helped in the training of the city folk. Numbers were slowly rising along with morale, yet rumours had began to circulate of demons and other nasty creatures and of past battles. Blandithorpe had still not returned and Alanthos was beginning to feel that the gates would have to be shut and locked as the night sky drew in. Leaving it as long as he could, Alanthos eventually gave the command to lock the gates; their heavy wooden block was secured and the city became secure for the night. The city folk settled down to as normal life as they could, all except the sentries that were posted at the towers watching in every direction for signs of life.

Blandithorpe and Kandibuck had travelled steadily all day and now they watched the sun drop slowly in the horizon, its rays causing shadows to spread their mark over the rough terrain. On several occasions Blandithorpe had stopped, sure that he had seen movement, but every time proved false and Kandibuck was getting tired of his paranoia. Blandithorpe gestured for them to stop, then indicated that they look over towards a small stony outcrop. Kandibuck looked then turned to continue.

"There, over there, behind that rock."

"Will you stop! You'll have me believing before long."

Kandibuck spoke in a sarcastic and spiteful manner, but stopped short as he thought he might have seen something too. Blandithorpe had headed towards the rocks before he could indicate that he may have also. Blandithorpe seemed to be deliberately heading into trouble and Kandibuck needed to stop him. Moving quickly, he headed to get between him and the rock formation but he was too slow. Blandithorpe was not disappointed as the leathery men ambushed them both. It all happened very fast and as Kandibuck went for his sword Blandithorpe had indicated not to and had allowed the capture. The lizard men were thin creatures, hard skinned through living in the swamps for such a long time. Their bodies were developed for water with long, wiry, strong arms and legs that ended in long sharp talons for gripping and manoeuvring in the moist conditions.

The lizard men bound them roughly then directed them along a narrow path partially hidden between two rocks; this soon dissipated into a shallow marsh and then into a boggy land. As they travelled Blandithorpe tried to reassure Kandibuck that he was in control of the situation. The deeper they went the worst the bog became; Kandibuck was finding staying on his feet difficult and stumbled several times only to be grasped roughly by the lizard men and righted, then pushed on. Blandithorpe was still showing some confidence that he was in control and was trying to reassure Kandibuck when suddenly, out of nowhere, a small cave entrance appeared. Before any communication could be made, Blandithorpe and Kandibuck were pushed roughly from behind into the darkness. Just as their eyes began to get accustomed to the dark they found themselves in a small set of corridors, then pushed into a smaller room and the huge door slammed shut. Blandithorpe screamed after his foes to no avail and Kandibuck just stared into the dark crossly.

"We need to talk, we need your help, listen to me."

The lizard men disappeared, leaving both alone in the small damp cell. Kandibuck slowly turned to look harshly at Blandithorpe.

"Well done, Sir, now what do you suggest?"

His tone was one of disgruntle and his body language was the same.

Looking around as their eyes adjusted to the light, the room was small yet had a small rock in the corner to sit on. There was no window and only the door had a small opening at eye level that let the small amount of light in. Blandithorpe moved to the door and peered out: just outside and to the right of the door was a younger lizard man who sat uncomfortably watching the cell, his eyes yellow shining in the little light and darting back and forth up the corridors. It was a good hour before any noise was heard of any approach; the lizard man rose from his seat quickly and straightened his clothes. It was the first time that Blandithorpe realised that the man wore only thin scaly armour made from what looked like fish skin. The lizard shifted awkwardly and waited the arrival.

Shortly, three other lizard men, two young and one older, dressed in finer armour of a good quality scale approached and were greeted by a strange salute where the young guard threw his long arm up straight above his head while giving a shrill quick whistle, then in one swift move bent the top of his arm to hit his chest. This was mimicked by the younger two and acknowledged by the elder. Upon reaching the guard, one of the two young lizard men spoke in a quick rasping tongue unknown to either captured man. The door was then opened and into the small damp room came the three and the door was shut quickly behind. One held a weakly flickering torch that barely lit the holder's features, covering no other area at all. The elder lizard spoke once again in the fast rasping tone and waited for a response, then spoke again to one of the others who bowed slightly and turned to Blandithorpe and Kandibuck, speaking in a very disjointed and slow fashion with a low rasping tone.

"I speak little human, why no fight capture?"

The lizard watched the men curiously as he waited for the answer.

Kandibuck sat on the stone and watched the whole thing through angry eyes. Blandithorpe rose slowly and, moving in a deliberately slow fashion, spoke slowly back to the lizard man.

"I am Blandithorpe of Whiteceder and this is Kandibuck. We have come for help. Our village was attacked by orcs and they will attack again."

As he spoke he showed his battle worn clothes and injuries. The three lizard men listened in silence, searching the faces of the men for hidden thoughts. Once Blandithorpe had finished, the lizard man turned to the elder lizard and spoke rapidly in the rasping language again. The lizard listened then spoke back to the younger. A smile crossed the lizard's face as he spoke, then the lizard turned to face the men once again. As he spoke the other young lizard man drew his sword, a crude looking bladed weapon and he did also.

"We not help... we okay thank you."

Turning to leave, the elderly lizard moved towards the door, the other two blocking the exit guardedly with their swords. Knocking, the door was opened and the same salute given by the guard before the three left the cell. Once through the cell was shut tightly again, and the three headed off back up the corridors into the dark. Blandithorpe rushed to the door and screamed out of the small hole.

"We need your help, don't you understand?"

Once the three had disappeared from view Kandibuck stood and threw a punch squarely on the jaw of Blandithorpe.

"You fool, why did I follow you... why?"

Both sat back down on the damp stone in painful silence, Blandithorpe nursed his jaw and thought deeply about their choices.

Outside, in view and out of reach, were their weapons. The guard was near and alert to them both.


Xendon sat in the outer chamber of the magnificently decorated chapel. Held in his hand was a small cloth sack; for the last hour he had collected various plants that he could use in creating defensive weapons against any attack. These were varying in shapes and colours. Sitting with him was the head Zenithe temple worshipper and Xendon spoke in hushed tones, explaining the various uses. The Zenithe listened closely without interrupting, but his face on more than one occasion had showed discontent. Out of the sack Xendon took an oval shaped hairy bulb with an orange tint. Along its surface were lots of odd lumps and to one end was a long root that was covered in long thin tentacle-looking roots. Xendon spoke once again, in hushed tones so as not to offend the temple worshippers. As he did he held the plant delicately.

"This plant is one of the most diverse plants I know." Smiling he continued. "The Inkopidian is not only a delicious vegetable, but has various other properties to it."

Dipping the bulb in a small bowl of water that he had placed near him on the step while talking, he lifted the bulb out and showed it to the Zenithe. As soon as the bulb hit the water the lumps opened to take in the water. Xendon took the bulb and squeezed it tight in his skilled hands; black ooze dripped from the openings. The Zenithe watched intently in silence as the ooze was very carefully collected by Xendon on a large waxy leaf, then the edges were turned to cover the ooze that Xendon cautiously placed into the cloth sack.

"This liquid can be used to dye certain materials, once dry in will be perfectly safe and slightly waterproof. However, while in the damp form it takes on another form."

Standing, Xendon indicated that he wished the Zenithe to follow. Turning, he made his way to the nearest exit. Once outside he turned towards the allotment to the right of the temple. Searching out a small cabbage, he plucked it neatly from the ground then walked to an open area before placing the cabbage down. Then Xendon reached into the sack and took the waxy leaf out again. Squeezing the leaf gently, he allowed a few drops of the black ooze to fall onto the cabbage. Then once the leaf was safe back in his sack he backed away to where the Zenithe stood.

"Watch carefully."

As Xendon spoke he took his staff from his back where it had been fastened by a leather belt and pointed the white stone at the top of the staff at the cabbage. Speaking slowly, he concentrated on the cabbage and spoke the incantation. The stone glowed brilliantly then fired off in the direction of the cabbage a small bright flame that engulfed the cabbage in the flame. As the flame hit the cabbage there was instantly a massive explosion; bits of cabbage went everywhere. The noise and dust was immense and several seconds passed before the large hole in the dirt could be seen where the cabbage had once stood.

The Zenithe looked on in horror and stared in disgust for several seconds before speaking.

"We are a peaceful race. We only defend the Source, not attack."

Xendon lost the excited smile quickly as he turned towards the Zenithe.

"Sometimes needs must, peace has a price," was all he said in an apologetic fashion.


The sound of a distinctive low horn broke the conversation abruptly; Xendon apologised then turned and ran in the direction of the horn. The horn was that of the sentry on the watchtower and meant someone was approaching. Upon arriving at the tower the guard, a young man in plate armour covered in the cloth of the Greatoak insignia, called down to him, the wind twisting the oak on his chest awkwardly.

"Armies approach and large ones, Sir."

Xendon acknowledged the guard then rallied the city folk around and began calming the confusion before giving orders of defensive nature. Once finished, he then made his way up the tower to see for himself the army approaching. What his eyes beheld was more than his mindset had been and had a sickening effect on his stomach.

For as far as the eye could see were creatures all marching as one towards the city walls: trolls pushing heavy climbing gear and banging war drums, orcs and goblins in tight packs moving in and out all armoured and heavily armed, and also in the sky flew a few flying lizards, their sharp eyes and claws at the ready. The sky was red and swirling with dark black clouds that threatened heavy rain, and smoke was rising from various vantage points where a village was under attack. The only light was that of occasional lightning that fell in a destructive fashion. The young guard was beside himself and Xendon tried to reassure him before returning his gaze to the horror before him.

"Where are Shadma, Tinden, and Blandithorpe?" Xendon spoke to himself as he watched the vast armies.

Shadma had set a fierce pace that Tinden had kept up with for a long time before needing the occasional break; when needed he climbed onto the broad back of Shadma and joined his pack. Shadma was coping with the journey with no real problems and seemed to be enjoying himself. The journey had been all on an upward incline and had slowly lost the beauty of the country and turned into wilderness, and then the wilderness thinned out to be replaced with hills and finally mountains. The air was getting thin and the wind fresh, to the point of cutting into the very soul, freezing your blood, so Tinden had felt. Shadma didn't seem to notice and cheerfully continued on his way.

On the horizon could be seen a stretch of orangey mountain terrain as Shadma turned once again to speak to Tinden, who lay half exhausted on his back, pressed hard into him for warmth.

"A few more hours then we will be sat eating a warm broth with Maxinton. It's been a while but I am sure my cousin will welcome us."

Shadma spoke trying to control his voice yet Tinden sensed the unease in his tone.

It was dark when Blandithorpe awoke to the screams of battle. Sitting up, he saw Kandibuck already awake, trying to see what was happening through the small opening. Outside the cell there was complete uproar. The guard had left his post and their weapons and had joined the scene outside, the air was fresh with the smell of orc, and the sound of battle was unmistakable. Blandithorpe rose quickly and barged the door; the door took the blow well but budged a little. Ignoring the jarred muscles he barged again, this time with Kandibuck. Two more attempts and the door gave enough to allow the escaping of one individual at a time. Grabbing their swords, they ran up the corridors towards the noise. Once outside the evening light still hurt for a few seconds. Once their eyes adjusted, before them was a battle between the lizard men and a small army of orcs. The orcs were highly trained and the lizards had taken quite a battering.

Kandibuck let out a yell with a passion only a long-suffering soldier could give. His blade swung wide, cutting two orcs as they attacked some lizard men. Both fell hard to the floor, and in the next movement another took the sting from his blade. Blandithorpe used his heavy broad sword with such ease that it could have been made of plastic. The orcs soon fell back and began aiming their attention to the soldiers not so much the lizard men; sweat poured from both as they fought on slowly, then the number attacking took its toll and both became tired. Kandibuck took a severe blow to his back and spun awkwardly to the floor then was sliced in half by another. Blandithorpe saw the opportunity and in the confusion dived into a bush followed by two orcs; one swung his crooked sword catching Blandithorpe in the back with a long yet not to deep wound.

Blandithorpe landed heavy but forced himself to roll over onto the cut to defend himself against the orc. A lizard man followed and began killing both with some ease while Blandithorpe lay low to gather his strength. Soon after killing the orcs, the lizard disappeared back through the opening, leaving him to rest in secret. Most of the orcs had already died or left and soon the noise level dropped. Blandithorpe slowly edged to the opening in the bush and, looking out, was confronted by a sword that narrowly missed him. Turning, he fought the two orcs that stood there.

After, Blandithorpe stood, his arms on fire, his lungs screaming at him. Sweat poured out under his tunic and his armour was damaged, yet he was all alone and able to rest. Looking around, the carnage was immense. Slowly, he moved to where Kandibuck lay in a heap. Lifting his body, he laid it in a natural way and then placed his sword, still gripped tightly in his dead arm, onto his chest with both arms holding it and the blade covering his face. Standing, Blandithorpe bowed to his companion, then swiftly turned and set off in a southerly direction to gather help if he could.

Mutley's keen eyes were scanning the mist for any sign of danger; the mist was so thick now that seeing more than a few feet ahead took concentration. Having travelled only an hour from the Devil's Entrance, the world seemed a totally different place. The slate walls were high and precariously balanced; the light was sifted badly and took on the appearance of evening. What sun got through had little if any strength. The way ahead was becoming a narrow gravelly road, and the dust helped to encourage even more difficulty in seeing anything. Slassiantha had slowed her pace unintentionally and was studying Kerstan's back as he walked along watching everywhere. The air was very thin and encouraged sleepy thoughts, so Slassiantha whistled gently to herself to keep alert.

"There will do to camp. It is sheltered and may be dry."

Mutley spoke as he scurried around the little vegetation for firewood. His eyes stayed ever watchful. Slassiantha took the opportunity to check Kerstan's wound; although it seemed to trouble him it was healing extremely fast and with no infection. As Slassiantha bathed the wound she was amazed at the rate the pink flesh was appearing. Kerstan moved away slightly and was caught by Slassiantha, who pulled him back.

"Why are you so interested in my wound?" His words were a little stern yet questioning.

"The healing is incredible so clean and quick."

Slassiantha spoke quietly and smiled as she spoke, her eyes rarely leaving his wound to search his eyes. Kerstan seemed to smirk a little before answering.

"Wounds heal well on me, they always have as far as I remember."

Slassiantha stopped bathing the wound and seemed to think for a while. As she continued she absently started again. "Do you remember why my mum and dad were banished?" Her voice started to waver with the memory.

Kerstan shook his head and shrugged. "No, that always puzzled me. I became ill, then they left."

Slassiantha seemed to toy with the next sentence and smiled to herself. "This may sound silly, Mum and Dad gave you a blood transfusion."

"What? So."

"Well it was shortly after that, that they were taken."

Kerstan studied Slassiantha before answering. "I needed it, so what is the problem?"

Slassiantha moved nervously as she spoke. "I am not certain but I think a Catcher was involved."

Kerstan stiffened as he spoke; his face was one of stone. "No. Your parents worked alone, you must be wrong."

Both had sat in silence as Mutley built and started a small fire, the small amount of vegetables he had found were boiling before Kerstan spoke again.

"The blood!" He screwed his face up in disgust. "No way, that thought is ridiculous."

Kerstan, however, thought about his strange idea over the meal. It would explain his movement and reactions and the healing, no, he would not accept that he took blood from a Catcher.

As the light was getting too bad to continue, after the meal plans were made to take turns in keeping watch and their beds were made. Before long, Mutley and Slassiantha were asleep. Kerstan could not sleep even if he had wanted to. All around took on an eerie silence and the feeling that he was being watched would not leave.


The wind had picked up and seemed to bite into Theorn as he sat high in one of the watchtowers; along with him were a few city folk, the majority of whom were untrained and looked worriedly out at the approaching menace. It would be several hours before the first attack, yet the battle drums were easily heard giving their ominous warning. Alanthos was gathering young and able men and was training them in the art of battle. The city was becoming prepared.

Theorn looked down on the city and all was a hustle and bustle. Although there were a vast amount of folk, would it be enough? he thought to himself. Turning from the scene, he forced his eyes back to the gathering armies outside. The rain was now in the air and the first few drops could be felt, not long before the downpour that was certain to follow. Xendon was standing near a small cart, which held a few cages with chickens in. Children had gathered as he waved his hands creating small coloured sparks that danced to their delight, their laughter a pleasant relief in the present atmosphere. The women continued to go about their daily life to create as normal a life for the others, cooking fresh bread and cakes, the smell drifting around the grounds in the wind.

The weather was turning cold and the sky had an unusual red to it as Blandithorpe started off, however he had to continue. Refusing to look back at the carnage, he made his way towards the border lands to the south, there he would find help. Barrenbar was a merchant's town and held plenty of highly dangerous types, trained and for hire. The journey would take most of the night but sleep would have to wait. The cut was bleeding and may need further care, but that would wait also. Slowly and deliberately he moved off at a steady pace. The path ahead was not proving a nice one.

Shadma and Tinden were both glad to see the mountains begin to diminish as the snow began to settle. A lone wolf studied them from a distance before leaving the way it had come. A crisp layer of pure white snow, being of a flat nature, had gathered in places, and a small mound already covered the land sheltered by the mountains. A narrow lane led down in a shallow gradient and was cut in two by a half frozen stream, then beyond the lane continued to a point where it forked to the right and led to what looked like a village of stone.

The village itself was of a fine sculptured nature, cut directly into the rocky landscape, rising to at least three times the height of Shadma at times. It looked as naturally part of the land as the mountains that surrounded it. The buildings all stood as if part of the land, and consisted of a large hall big enough to house two inns from the city, and also several other buildings that housed the giants that lived there. There was also a smaller building that held a few cattle that grazed happily on some hay. Their approach had been noticed by two large giants wearing guards' uniforms. Shadma smiled and acknowledged them with a jovial wave, continuing towards the village. Tinden drew back a little at the size of the guards yet stayed close to Shadma.

The guards stood blocking the entrance to the village. Their arms held heavy maces and they looked menacingly at Shadma and Tinden.

"Who goes there?"

Shadma continued to advance slowly and motioned to Tinden to follow.

"It is I, Shadma O'Rhathhauz, returned to speak to the King."

The guard nearest seemed to recognise him for the first time, and a cruel smile crossed his lips before he answered.

"Been a long time Shadma 'lover o' humans' Rhathhauz. Maxinton will be pleased to see you again."

The guards had already closed off the exit when they first spoke. Shadma and Tinden then were showed roughly into the village.


The walls of the city seemed to shake under the sound of the battle drums. Theorn and Alanthos watched from the tower as the vast army approached, stopping just out of arrow range. The rain fell now in thick sheet form, covering the ground. The ground soon became unable to swallow the water and puddles started to gather. Lightning fell all around, the sky was a deep red and the smell of fire was strong in the air. The city folk had been gathered into small groups and were scattered over the battlements, armed with bows the arrows cocked and ready. On the ground inside other groups waited, some with pikes, others on horseback. Xendon was throwing orders at them and trying to keep the calm. A horse began to buck and was quickly brought back under control.

The creatures came at the walls in one terrible swoop of violent action. Their black leathery bodies were a blur as they rushed the walls; from the battlements the first rally of arrows was sent. The arrows flew at the mass and accuracy was not an issue, several creatures fell but the effect was so little to make an effect. The city folk began to panic and only Alanthos's highly trained skill kept control. Trolls had pushed through the mass and were putting the climbing gear in place. Theorn called for the oil in large containers on the battlements to be poured onto the gear. Theorn then lit a torch and let it drop onto the climbing gear; flames and smoke rose and the heat was soon unbearable. The gear was abandoned and another was pushed up to replace it. The smoke became worse as the air took hold of the oil, rain having little effect on dousing the flames.

Xendon reached into his pack and produced the black ooze in its leaf; dipping cloth in the ooze he then wrapped another over and lit it, then threw it quickly over and into the mass below. Large explosions threw the orcs in all directions. One of the lizards flew in to attack, its huge frame blotting out the light. Razor sharp claws tore at its victims as it flew off again. Several men fell from the battlements in the attack. The lizard (a Drarghen) swooped down again; Xendon threw a piece of soaked cloth at it. The Drarghen caught the cloth and knocked two more down then turned to leave again. Theorn fired a flaming arrow as the lizard flew overhead; instinctively the lizard caught it and was thrown awkwardly off into the mass below. Its body was torn apart: its lower half was in tatters and it lay convulsing on the floor before dying. Still the creatures came, and the walls were beginning to be scaled. It would not be long, thought Theorn, as he fired accurate arrows down into the fray.


Slassiantha had stood and listened, straining her eyes in the dark for what seemed like minutes. Her eyes ached and her ears were numb but she was certain that she had heard Clickers approaching. Shaking Kerstan, who was instantly erect with his sword drawn, she then turned to Mutley and pointed in the direction. Mutley had woken more slowly, and rubbing his eyes he drew his sling also. It took only a short while before the party saw the yellow eyes. Several pairs were moving in their direction cautiously. Mutley tossed onto the fire some dry roots that hissed then lit, throwing enough light to see their attackers. Eight Clickers skulked in the dark in their direction, and as soon as the light hit them they lunged at the party.

Kerstan's reaction's allowed him to stand in the way and chop the nearest. Mutley took a flaming twig and moved towards the creatures, while Slassiantha made her way to go around them. Four attacked Kerstan, who cut two down before being knocked to the floor. Rolling, he regained his footing and started attacking again. Mutley was managing to keep the Clickers at arm's length, but their sharp teeth snapped at the twig all the same.

Slassiantha managed to move around slightly before the Clickers noticed her moving. The two remaining moved to stop her path, and Slassiantha, her sword in her one hand, raised the other. A familiar feeling rushed over her body bathing her in warmth, and a boulder around eight inches square shot from the floor at a fast speed and spun off the head of one Clicker. The Clicker shook its head then glanced over its shoulder. The movement was enough for Slassiantha to slice the creature with her sword. The other was held at bay by the wide arc of her swipe.

Kerstan was in a frenzy of action, his muscles moving at such speed the Clickers that fought him were struggling to make contact. One took a blow to the ribs and landing awkwardly, rolling to its feet again; the other locked its teeth into his trousers only to be knocked free and stabbed with such speed and power that the sword blade went right up to the hilt. Kerstan withdrew with the same speed and was ready to attack again. One Clicker was alight and continued to attack Mutley as he swung wildly with the twig, its flame almost out. The other had joined the attack of Kerstan. Mutley was in a panic and swung frantically in all directions that helped to keep the creature away until it collapsed with the flame finishing it off.

With just a few left, the Clickers turned and ran back into the mist. Panting heavily, Kerstan turned to try to calm the now crazed person near him. Mutley was shaking vigorously and breathing quickly, his face full of fear.

"We will have to move on. They will be back with more."

Kerstan spoke in an angry voice that broke through the barrier that Mutley had built around himself. Mutley stared out into the mist and slowly, without taking his eyes off the mist, moved off. It took Mutley several minutes before his tracking instincts calmed him again.

The party travelled on for the next hour with no other incident; slowly along with the first light their security of each other returned. As the light returned the high slate mountains became visible again, the mist was still heavy on the ground but vision was easier. Slowly, the party returned to the routine of 'follow my leader'. The surroundings were still much the same. It was Slassiantha who first heard the sound.

As Mutley had picked up the pace again and Kerstan had started to show little pain from his wound, Slassiantha had indicated to slow and then all heard the sound. From behind a high slate hill it had started at a low level, and as they approached the sound became louder. The sound was peculiar and sounded like a large bird in distress, yet also like a young girl's voice and the familiar sound of Clickers. Slowing their pace, they made their way to look down on the incident.

Upon reaching the top of the rock, Kerstan and Slassiantha looked on the odd scene. Several Clickers were snapping and lunging at a young bronze-coloured girl of around fourteen who was on the back of a large bird. The bird looked much like a hawk yet was as big as a baby elephant. The girl looked at one with the bird as it flapped wildly and tried to fly with its leg caught in a net. The young girl was fighting from the back using an axe with such a powerful talent that the bird was able to flap freely; the Clickers seemed unable to penetrate her attacks yet were cunning enough to dodge in and out to try to tire her, then kill both the bird and the girl. Mutley soon joined Kerstan and Slassiantha and looked on the scene also.

"Zinobian and her Roc. Let them have her."

His voice was one of contempt and he turned to leave. Slassiantha grabbed hold of his arm, turning him angrily around. Kerstan looked on in both wonder and disbelief.

The strategies used by Theorn and Alanthos had so far held off the creatures but their numbers were too high. Several orcs had managed to climb the walls only to be knocked off either on their way up or as they crossed the battlements. The smoke from the fires was becoming a thick mass and caused both frustration and difficulty breathing. The city folk were also finding it difficult to see the many creatures below as they made their attacks on the walls. Some leathery trolls lumbered up to the gates and began pounding on the gates; each blow shook the gates but both the locks and hinges held. The rain was coming down heavier and was beginning to extinguish the flames. Xendon wrapped his robe tighter around himself in an attempt to hold the rain off and rushed past the city folk that were shooting arrows and tossing rocks down on the creatures. Finding the stairs, he made his way down quickly and went to the gates; there he began helping in adding to the blockage with extra metal rods. The gates shook violently yet still held.

In the chapel the Source glowed at a violent rate. Its power to help the struggle to survive was needed more each second; small lumps of its honeycomb were decaying and holes were appearing in the fragile frame. The Zenithe worked hard with the magic to repair and restore the Source. The Source had been created to provide health and protection but decay was setting in badly now.

Theorn began to feel despair as he looked upon the creatures. Letting several accurate arrows going into the fray helped the frown leave his face; all around him men were fighting as one to defend their homes. As Theorn drew his bow back once again his whole body tensed with fear; the fear was unnaturally strong. Looking around to see what may be causing this fear he saw three wild-cat-like creatures moving at an incredible pace. As the creatures moved the ground before them emptied of creatures: orcs, trolls and goblins alike ran in complete panic then returned slowly to join the battle. The Sleepers were determined, destroying all in their wake. Theorn turned and ran towards the main staircase. As soon as he reached it he yelled at the top of his voice.

"Sleepers! Control your fear!"

City folk were in every kind of panic: several lay curled in a tight ball, others ran to hide. Alanthos forced himself to stay calm and began getting the control back as quickly as he could.

"Calm yourselves. Back to the gates," he bellowed.

At that point the gates gave an immense shake and a small crack

began to appear in the frame holding their hinges. Several men ran to aid holding the gate. Xendon appeared from somewhere and rushed past the commotion; his face was tense and full of determination. Up the stairs he went and to the battlements. Frenzied screams could be heard from the Sleepers outside as they bashed the gates repeatedly. Fighting to control his shaking hands, Theorn shot three arrows off in quick succession, each hitting their target. The Sleepers by now were an easy target as all other creatures had fled the area and were standing some way off. Each arrow embedded itself deep into a Sleeper.

One Sleeper stopped its attack on the gate and stared up at Theorn, locking its gaze on him. Fear beyond any that Theorn had ever coped with tore into every fibre of his mind. Theorn flung himself backwards and lay screaming on the floor, rolling around like a mad man. Several men went to his aid, preventing him hurting himself. Upon reaching the top, Xendon plunged his hand deep into his robe and produced a small box; his face was not focusing on anything and a look of total panic was present. Taking the box he threw it down at the Sleepers, then sent a ball of fire from his hand down into the Sleepers. The flame wrapped itself around the Sleepers and the box and the black liquid inside it.

BOOM!

Bits of Sleeper along with rock and wood went everywhere. The gate splintered and threw wood in towards the men; several collapsed under the wood, others were thrown, hurt badly and burnt by the explosion. Men, women, and children lay dead or dying everywhere. Xendon suddenly realised what he had done, his mind clearing as the fear disappeared. The Sleepers were gone but at what price? The gate hung awkwardly on its hinges and the carnage was everywhere. People were already trying to repair the gates, but outside the creatures were already heading to enter the opening and invade. Alanthos grabbed the reins of a horse and mounted it quickly. Pushing through the crowd, he took a large army of men to defend as attempts to repair the foundations took place.

"For the Source and the city!" he yelled.

The army responded as if in an echo and pressed on to stop the onslaught. Theorn was on his feet and lunged at Xendon, knocking him to the ground; men dragged them apart. Xendon slowly rose to his feet and looking around in total despair and disbelief. He turned and left towards the chapel at a pace. Theorn spat on the floor as he went, then turned to defend the battlements once again.

Alanthos rode his horse hard into the fray; taking his lead the men did as well. The orcs were taken off guard by the speed of attack and were knocked back. The Source glowed brighter. The men fought with vigour beyond normal and the creatures fell back. There were so many it seemed impossible, yet the men were accomplishing holding off the attack. Invisible helpers held the creatures at bay.


Blandithorpe, although aching all over, had not stopped. Sweat poured from him like a small stream. The merchant village of Barrenbar was close now, it's huge foreboding gate that had held out trouble over the years stood before him. Walls as high as ten feet spanned the horizon, not a welcoming sight for any passerby who may happen upon the village. Flying in the wind was the crest of Barrenbar, a gauntleted hand holding a mace and crossed by a spear with a dark red background. The occupants were all mercenaries and highly trained in various tasks, each skilled in their own trade and ready to serve the highest bidder. Blandithorpe did not slow as he made his way to the gate; upon reaching it he banged hard with his sword. A small opening appeared in the door and an ugly scarred face appeared. The man screwed his face and then smiled.

"Well if it isn't the squirt, come to see Buckenbear have you?"

Not waiting for the answer the gate opened.

Once inside the gate the village took on a busy appearance not much different to a seaport, everyone bustling around busy and ignoring the others. There was a massive armoury with weapons that many folk outside the walls would never have seen before. Each was immaculately made with such perfection that people travelled from far to buy the wears or to hire people who could use them. Carts that could withstand a fierce attack were being made and painted, each with great skill. Cattle wandered the ground freely, as did chickens.

Blandithorpe ignored the sight and pushed his way through the busy people towards a large building with smoke rising from its chimney. As he approached, his eyes took in the familiar back of his cousin. Buckenbear was not the average man: his broad shoulders were the envy of most and his arms were not to be ignored either. Clothed in the finest leather tunic soaked in sweat, he worked. The metal on the workbench took such a pounding from the hammer in his hand, yet each blow was with such skill that the metal formed a breastplate fit for one of the King's army. All around the walls hung finely made chain mail and other armour.

"Buckenbear you tyrant, got a minute?"

The shoulders and arms of the man stiffened slightly before relaxing again. Turning, Buckenbear held the look of a man to fear. Upon seeing Blandithorpe, the hammer held in his hand dropped unnoticed to the straw floor. Buckenbear smiled a broad smile fitting to his size.

His huge frame smothered Blandithorpe who felt his life being crushed out of him. Wincing from the cut, he floated in mid-air until being placed on the ground. Buckenbear had a face of concern, noticing for the first time the stains on his shirt. Holding Blandithorpe in his strong arms he studied the cut and frowned, muttering to himself. Turning, he placed Blandithorpe on the bench and then sat down next to him.

"What's happened to you?"

Conversation came fast and didn't slow for the next hour, Buckenbear slowly turning from worried for his cousin to angry for the city.

"There must be a few here that still regard the city highly enough to defend it." He spoke in an unsure fashion. "They will expect payment though."

He spoke as if to apologise yet shrugging all the same. Blandithorpe smiled and patted his cousin on the back before gingerly rising from the bench. Every bone ached from the journey and then the rest.

"Let's see old Idris. He'll patch you up."

Laughing, they both headed arm in arm towards a peculiar tent towards the centre of the village: the home of the travelling healer, one of the best witchdoctors in the area.

Kerstan and Slassiantha had both waited long enough; the girl needed help however skilled she was.

"That Roc is tiring, we need to move soon."

Slassiantha spoke in anger more than asking. Mutley had made it clear he was not going down to help any Zinobian young or old, and this only fuelled Slassiantha into action. Mutley was almost screaming at her although the volume was so little the effort seemed stupid.

"That is a Zinobian girl, have nothing to do with her." His total disgust shone brightly in every way humanly possible.

Gently rebuking him Kerstan spoke. "Zinobian or not, that girl needs our help. She fights like a demon possessed but is soon to tire."

Mutley sat heavily on the floor, crossing his bony arms and

spitting. He turned his head from both of them. Slassiantha was already moving slowly around the top of the rocks to make her way behind. Kerstan ignored Mutley and dashed out in full attack. The girl, although extremely exhausted, continued to fight every blow, knocking the frustrated Clickers away from her mount. The Roc flapped furiously, batting the Clickers to the ground as well as freeing her claw from the net inch by inch. Not an ounce of fear showed in the little girl's face, just pure hatred for the creatures before her. Her determination had won so far and would continue to for as long as it took.

The Clickers continued to snap here and there, backing off then re-attacking, not giving the girl time for rest. Their total concentration on the girl and the bird allowed Kerstan to be within striking distance before the first turned to defend. It was only instinct that saved the Clicker, a small cut under the ribcage oozed brown watery liquid. The face of the Clicker turned from shock to outrage; using its strong back legs it leapt towards Kerstan. Kerstan easily sidestepped then swung again. This time the blade connected better. One leg hung limp, the other had been cut off completely. The Clicker rolled in agony, thrashing at its opponent until the blade finished it once and for all. Now the Clickers turned their attention to the two foes, naturally dividing the attack without hesitation. Kerstan was in full attack and, using his speed and skill, began giving the girl the time she needed. The girl also used the advantage well, easily cutting the nearest in half then the net near the claw of the Roc.

Slassiantha closed her eyes and concentrated: the feeling of warmth was returning. Opening her eyes, she directed the power into the area in front of her. A huge fiery yellow flame beast appeared: its hairy body was pure fire and it stood ten feet tall. The arms and legs were huge with powerful talons, and grabbing the nearest Clicker the beast crushed it without trouble then threw it aside, turning to the next. The Clickers began attacking in all directions, not sure who was the bigger threat. The nearest dodged a swing from Kerstan and narrowly missed scratching his arm, diving aside it rolled then attacked again. The girl continued to slash at the netting and the Clickers with the help of the Roc. Slassiantha swayed a little with perspiration appearing on her face, yet continued from her hiding place to direct the beast. The beast flickered but appeared again and continued the attack. Working together, it did not take long to beat the Clickers back into the mist. Most lay dead, one or two severely charred, most with bad cuts and gashes. Slassiantha closed her eyes again and felt dizzy, collapsing to the floor where she stood. Kerstan ran to her aid, cradling her head in his powerful arms. Looking around, he saw the bronzed girl rear her Roc into the air with little concern for them both. She was soon gone, out of sight over the slate banks, and all was silent again.

The mist was less heavy and the air was a little damp. Rain could be felt in the air. Several minutes had passed with Kerstan gently caressing Slassiantha's brow before she stirred. Slassiantha looked at Kerstan through tired, bleary eyes and a faint smile crossed her lips. Distracted by movement, Kerstan turned to see Mutley approaching slowly; his eyes were full of fear and he looked everywhere as he approached. The fiery beast had disappeared as soon as Slassiantha collapsed, but this did not ease Mutley's fears at all. Upon nearing them both Mutley began clapping them both in a sarcastic manner, his whole manner one of total disgust.

"You let her go! Fool, she will return and kill us all."

Kerstan looked from Slassiantha to Mutley then spat out the words, "What is done is done."

Mutley involuntarily stepped back a couple of steps before righting himself again. Kerstan returned his look after a few more seconds of hard stares at Mutley to the face of Slassiantha.

"What was that thing, where did it come from, why did it help?"

Slassiantha lay still for several seconds and Kerstan began to wonder if she had heard him or not. Slowly she took a deep breath and sighed. Looking from Kerstan to Mutley and back she spoke in a quiet tone.

"Magic, taught me by my mother."

Her voice was giving away her sorrow and wavered slightly. Kerstan brushed the hair out of Slassiantha's face and forced a smile, and then he gently sat her up and turned his attention back to Mutley.

"Gather our gear up. We're moving on."

Mutley looked at Kerstan in defiance, then quickly turned and picked up their packs. With ease, Kerstan helped Slassiantha to her feet then gently put his arm around her waist to help her move on. Slassiantha gently pushed his arm away and gestured she was alright to continue alone. Reluctantly Kerstan moved away and, keeping half an eye on her, set off once again.

Slassiantha spoke anxiously to Kerstan, her voice taut. "Please tell no one of this, I would be banished."

"We are well into the mountains so not long now," he said, as much for his own benefit as theirs to cover the conversation, giving her a gentle squeeze in answer then was quiet once again. All around them hung high black ledges of slate, the vegetation had become sparser and the mist was returning. Gentle rain broke through the high walls. Grudgingly the party moved on.

Alanthos turned his horse back through the ranks and shouted instructions to the men. Looking around him, he could see through the heavy rain that the small army were gaining ground, how he was not sure but ground was gained. Sending a young man back he gave orders that a small group of horsemen were needed to encircle the orcs and attack from the side. The man dashed off back towards the gates. By now repairs were being made and the gates would withstand a small attack, but for how long?

The battle continued with both sides taking casualties, a horn sounded from the battlements and several horsemen left the gates at a pace. Around one hundred men bravely pushed their horses out to meet the vast armies before them. They had to attempt to delay the attack. Kicking the horses into action, they moved around the army then charged full on into the fray. Alanthos joined them and gave an almighty war cry. Pikes down, the men forced the creatures into defensive action, pushing them back. This was temporary and soon they returned, on and on this went, both losing troops. Down to eighty-three horsemen they bravely attacked once again. Circling the many creatures they cut them down.

The Source glowed brightly and the Zenithe worked like they had never done before. More decay was appearing; the Zenithe showed signs of worry yet fought on in the attempt to heal and re-gathering supplies. Several more attacks occurred from the horsemen; archers had joined in as the creatures forced the battle closer to the battlements. Hope was beginning to diminish when, from over a hill to the south-east, a low strange horn was heard. Several orcs looked in the direction, fear in their eyes, recognition on their faces.

They came fast, horsemen, just two hundred of them but heavily armoured in fine armour. Each was holding weapons that were unseen by many, just as fine as the armour. Their horses were armoured too, the legs the only part totally unprotected. Blandithorpe was with them along with Buckenbear, their horses moving at the front. Battle cries rang in the air and chaos was to follow soon after; each man had a determined look, no fear at all. The first orcs took the wrath of the mercenaries and died quickly, and within seconds the group were in the middle of the vast armies, fighting hard. Heavily outnumbered, they fought, though the effect was not to their usual standard or liking.

Snode's heavy armour clanged as he took to his war horse: the time to join his armies in battle had come. His red molten skin showed clearly under his armour, talons shining with an eerie glow held the reins, and his eyes burned with hate. His huge frame was perched safely in a huge saddle and the horse, although massive, seemed to stagger slightly under the weight. His long tail with the venomous spikes lay gently over the flanks of the horse. Hanging attached to the bridle was Snode's staff, a twisted ash branch, heavily decaying and withered, with a thick spiny bramble crushed tightly around its frame.

With a gentle nudge that seemed unnatural to him, he guided the horse out from its resting place. Once out in the open, he gazed longingly on his troops, for as far as the eyes could see huge war trolls with thick leathery skins stood among orcs and goblins. Drarghens flew the sky, watching the creatures with mixed feelings of hunger and fellowship. Leathery men were among them also. Each and every one had been gathered over the years and prepared in private for this day. Huge cages held Sleepers that fought the bars in anticipation, bent on destruction and the need to kill magic, controlled by magic more evil than themselves. An evil smile swept the face of Snode and a cackle left the pit of his stomach. He was ready; the time had come to take back what his parents had fought for.

Sitting tall on the war horse's back, he took the staff in his taloned hand. An eerie glow instantly appeared over the staff that intensified each second. The ground near him began to crack and decay, and he lifted the staff high above his head. With a load roar he spoke, telling his troops to take the city, kill them all, and then destroy the Source, to let no one stand against them. As he spoke great bolts of fire redder than the volcano's core shot from his staff and filled the sky. The clouds darkened and split open, hurling rain at the troops below; lightning flashed around them. When Snode finished shouting his war cry the troops cried as one in reply. Their cheers rang out an awesome sound, filling the land around with fear. The skies got redder and darker and more lightning fell as the troops started towards the city.

The mountains hung heavy over Mutley, displaying his thoughts well. He had said very little to Kerstan or Slassiantha after his outburst over the Zinobian girl. He had kept a sharp eye on both as well as the area as he trudged on. The ground was getting rough and a small incline meant the light had diminished slightly; concentration crossed his already angry face. Several times Kerstan had caught him giving him a distasteful glance, and each had been ignored. The atmosphere was a damp and cold one, and the drizzle had not slowed so their clothes hung on them in a damp fashion. The road was getting narrower and before long the party had to walk in single file. Mutley took the lead and slowed, checking the ground and surrounding areas more and more as he went on. Kerstan had taken the rear to allow protection for Slassiantha, who had recovered her little weariness. Kerstan stopped suddenly and spoke in a whisper to the others.

"I feel others near."

He watched everywhere as he spoke. Mutley said they all felt the same but moved on slowly anyway. After a short while the road widened slightly and in the distance was a fork in the road. To the left it was narrow again and crossed a chasm that dropped several hundred feet, to the right it dipped considerably and became darker as it went on.

"Which way, Mutley?" Kerstan asked in a kindly fashion, waiting for an answer.

Mutley grunted at him yet replied, "Either is treacherous. One's shorter but over a chasm where ambush is rife, the other... well the other would add a day or two."

As he spoke, Mutley eyed the right path worriedly then looked towards the left. Kerstan looked at both but moved slowly in the left direction taking the lead. Mutley dropped to the back.

Kerstan edged forward and entered the narrow entrance to the chasm. The footing became dangerously loose and rubble fell on several occasions, each time the stones did not seem to sound at the bottom and the bottom could not be seen. Slowly he edged forward and had got just under halfway when he saw the movement. Moving at a pace from above him, hanging to the wall by its fingers, was a Clicker. Three others were close behind. A stone whizzed past him and the Clicker lost its grip, plunging into the darkness. A strange scream slowly disappeared along with the creature.

Drawing his sword, Kerstan edged forward and attacked the other Clickers; Slassiantha and Mutley stayed close with their weapons out too. Mutley reloaded and shot another stone off at the nearest.

Leaping, one Clicker flew at Kerstan, who barely managed to knock him aside without joining him in the fall. Further they pushed along the chasm; several more Clickers appeared from the slate. The chasm curved slightly and as Kerstan turned the corner to his horror on the other bank stood twenty or so Clickers. Attached to a huge chained harness, two held a huge longhaired matted black animal with a huge gaping ugly-toothed permanent smile of razor sharp teeth. The War Demon gave a crazed cry and began dragging the two attached Clickers in his direction.

Kerstan stopped and, still attacking the Clickers near him, slowly pushed Slassiantha and Mutley back. A Clicker left the wall and attacked Kerstan as another dropped, blocking the exit. Mutley turned and tried to back away as the Clicker attacked. Slassiantha raised her hand and the Clicker seemed to stop and then totter on the edge before falling over. More were coming and although Kerstan seemed to be able to keep them at bay as they edged back, there were too many. Then, around the corner moving at an incredible pace the Demon came, released from the Clickers. Slate in large quantities began falling all around and the ground shook gently as a small, then larger crack appeared in the chasm before the Demon.

Slassiantha stumbled and Mutley grabbed at her as she fell, his grip only had her by her arm and she swung wildly. Mutley held on and dug his feet into whatever he could. Desperately he hung on. The Demon had lunged and had fallen down the hole; Kerstan had heard the scream and turned to see Slassiantha fall. Clickers still came so he returned his attention to them yet the fallen slate blocked the way considerably. Kerstan knocked the two remaining off then turned his attention to the aid of a very tired Mutley who was holding Slassiantha who seemed to be unconscious. Slowly they both helped her back to the solid ground. Suddenly Kerstan felt a presence and, spinning with his sword that he had laid by his side to aid Mutley, he sliced a Clicker that had made his way over the rubble. The Clicker fell in surprise and was gone. Reluctantly the party made their way back to the fork.

"Was that you?" asked Kerstan, as he surveyed the area around them.

"Come on this way." Mutley spoke in a sharp tone and headed off down the right fork. Every few minutes he stopped and checked around, the further he went the more he stopped to examine the surroundings. Kerstan began watching him with a look of worried apprehension. The road dipped and as it did so the light did too. Mutley stopped again and checked the area thoroughly, looked back the way he had come – not for the first time – then reluctantly moved on. This was the pattern until in the distance the land became soggy to walk on and a large black opening was the only way forward. Mutley stopped again and began searching and looking around for something, looking back several times as if hoping to see an alternative way.

"Mutley, you have been acting like this for a while. What is wrong?" Slassiantha spoke suddenly, causing the already jumpy Mutley to dart away before he gained himself again. Mutley looked at them both, then at the jet-black entrance, then looked as if he wished to cry.

"What's in there?" Kerstan spoke this time, pointing at the entrance.

Mutley spoke, keeping his eyes firmly fixed away from the entrance, his voice wavering as he did. "Nothing... I... well it is dark in there."

Kerstan looked at Mutley with suspicion. "We have torches."

The reaction was quicker than expected, almost crying Mutley screamed uncontrollably. "NO! NOT TORCHES! THEY WILL SEE US!"

Suddenly realising his outburst, he looked away and kicked the floor nervously. Kerstan moved and touched Mutley on the shoulder. Mutley jumped yet looked at him anyway.

"What will?"

Mutley shrugged, swallowed hard then spoke again. "I... I don't really know but they are there... THEY ARE!"

His face was one of total terror. Kerstan looked at Mutley then Slassiantha. "We have no choice, we have to go in there for help for the city the other side!"


Shadma and Tinden had been led to a small room and told to wait; a guard was placed outside the room anyway. Several minutes had past and Tinden sat on the only chair in the room – a hard wooden chair; the only other furniture was a small table and a hung torch. Looking around the room, he wondered what Shadma had got him into, but time did not allow him to ponder on it for long. Into the room came two giants. Both wore armour of a dark golden colour and the second had a mean smile upon his face. Shadma, however, upon them entering smiled a big smile and went to hug the last, but was pushed aside by the first.

"So, the wanderer returns." Maxinton spoke in a cruel fashion and glared at Shadma, then turned his attention to Tinden. "So, not happy to embarrass us with just small folk, eh?"

The look he gave Tinden was one of contempt. Shadma just smiled in reply and spoke again. "Maxinton, it is good to see you. Don't hold my leaving against me."

The quick slap from the back of Maxinton's hand connected on Shadma's jaw. Blood trickled down his lip. Biting it hard, Shadma forced another smile. Tinden went to stand, but a look from Shadma stopped him. Shadma stood up tall, and being a head higher than both other giants, looked down on both then. He spoke again, this time with a little less friendliness.

"We need to talk over a matter of urgency."

Maxinton looked at Shadma and a wicked grin passed over his face then left as soon as it had passed.

"Yes we have got some catching up to do. Guards!"


Mutley looked at Kerstan and then at Slassiantha. Swallowing hard, he looked at the black entrance then unconsciously gave a glance backwards again before slowly moving towards the darkness. The closer they got to the entrance the darker it seemed to get inside, and upon reaching the entrance a musty smell issued from within. Kerstan lit a torch and ignored the protests coming from Mutley, who was edging away; his face still full of fear. Although burning brightly, the light did not give off a good light in the cave. Once inside, Kerstan stopped to look around. Slassiantha entered also, pushing Mutley before her. Stalactites and stalagmites hung as far as the light shone and the walls were slimy and wet; drips dropped from somewhere out of sight on regular intervals. On the wall, a few feet inside to the left, were strange drawings of weird looking people and a strange sort of ancient writing. Slassiantha held her torch closer and her eyes opened wide, her face screwed up in concentration while she studied the writing. Turning, she looked in the direction of Kerstan: only an outline was visible as he had moved to look at some odd shaped rocks nearby.

"The writing is an old tongue. I have seen it in some of my mother's books."

Kerstan turned and moved to look. "Have you any idea what it says?"

Slassiantha looked at Kerstan in an apologetic way, but spoke. "This symbol means to trap, this means magic, and that means to spoil... I think."

Kerstan looked as she pointed to various pictures and writing then shrugged. Mutley had his mouth wide open. His face was one of recognition.

"Yes, I thought I would remember given time." Kerstan looked at him and waited.

"The Tombs of the Tainted!"

Slassiantha stared in disbelief before speaking. "That was only a bedtime story told to scare us... Wasn't it?"

A story passed down from generation to generation, exaggerated here and there, but mostly the same...

Way back when dragons were plentiful and the land was full of magic and wonder, when every town and village had users of magic to keep the peace and defend against enemies, Catchers lived in huge herds freely; life was good in those days. Airored the Toothless had been an enlightened one for one of the great cities. He had called a conference between other enlightened ones in secret. Airored had practised magic for as long as memory allowed, under the wise teaching of Llahnsmead. Llahnsmead was faithful to the magic and taught well.

Airored had practiced alone and had wandered into forbidden territories. He had started small with making plants wither, but the power excited and the taint grew stronger. In a short while he practised more on his own than with Llahnsmead. On the day of the conference, Llahnsmead had been found burnt by magic and dead. Airored had gathered some of his faithful and had planned to rule. Great battles occurred, the lands as we know them had shifted in sympathy and many died and suffered under Airored. Airored, Handsmear the Terrible and the illusionist Dwain soon became names to fear.

After many years, those faithful to the true magic along with Yahyess, chief protector of the Catchers, met in secret then went to stop and defeat Airored and his Tainted. The battles had lasted for months; they were the worst battles, changing life as we had known it. Airored had summoned dragons to help and Yahyess had been forced to destroy them all, to virtual extinction. Airored and his faithful had been driven deep into the High Mountains, where they had hidden in a cave. Spies for Yahyess found and reported their whereabouts and a powerful spell was cast over the cave, blocking both entrances. The Tainted fought hard but lost the battle to leave the caves. However, the mountain changed and became as it is today. Slate as high as the sky, misty and evil: the Black Mountains. Stuck in the cave, the Tainted slowly died along with them their evil. It is said that all who go to the wrong magic are sent in their sleep to the tomb and there they stay.

Buckenbear threw his weight hard in the saddle, swinging the rear flank of his war horse into war. A troll stumbled yet kept his feet, only to be cut down by another horseman. The battle had stepped up a level and the fighting was fierce; archers fired their deadly arrows into the fray, taking great numbers with each volley. Theorn had sent another hundred out to join in defence and so far the defence held. The men gathered around and began to use their newly learnt skills to more effect; the creatures went into defence and drew back. The Source was glowing at an incredible brightness, the Zenithe were working in harmony with each other and all looked tired, yet they fought on. Slowly, the creatures took back the ground taken.

Trolls loaded great boulders of rock onto massive wooden catapults. The frame groaned under the weight then the ropes holding the slings were cut and the boulders flew high into the air towards the walls and towers of the city. One hit a tower and the rocks splintered like ten pins falling into the city grounds; cattle scattered or died in the carnage below, locked in the falling rocks by large fences. The impact was great and the Source reacted. One Zenithe gave a curdling cry and collapsed, holding its head and dying instantly. Another took its place and began repairing the already large damage showing.

Blandithorpe drove his horse through the mass of orcs; he had to get to those catapults. Two other mercenaries joined him, cutting the way forward to get to the trolls. The trolls turned, leaving the weapons and faced the oncoming horsemen. One mercenary swung deeply with his broadaxe, cutting the nearest troll. Only skill held him in his horse; the troll staggered but stayed on his feet. The second finished the first ones attack: one down and two to go. Blandithorpe yelled a war cry and throwing all his weight into the attack buried his sword deep into the back of another, leaving his horse with the force of the impact. The next troll fell. The battle took on yet another pace.

Shadma took the blow well and staggered but kept his feet; two large guards had taken him and Tinden, and under the watchful eye of Maxinton they began hitting and kicking them both. Tinden had only taken one blow before he collapsed in a heap; it was anger that held Shadma on his feet. Shadma lifted his massive arms and began to attack the guards also, the entire time calling to stop and that he needed to talk. The guards were large and strong but Shadma was bigger, not many giants had his bulk or determination. The first guard took the full force of his anger and spun in the air before coming to land heavily in a heap. The other hit Shadma with a club, stunning him. While Shadma was dazed the guard hit him again, knocking him to the floor. It was then that Maxinton waved for the guard to stop and kicked Shadma himself.

"Tie them up. Find out why they really have come."

Maxinton spoke without a hint of compassion for both then turned and walked off, leaving the guard to tie them. The other got to his feet, slowly rubbing his chin earnestly.

Kerstan looked at Mutley with concern.

"Well are you coming or do we go on alone?"

Mutley was standing as if part of the rock foundations themselves. Slowly he shook himself and nodded.

"Good, what about you?" Turning to Slassiantha he smiled reassuringly.

"We go on," she said, nodding. Kerstan took the lead and plunged into the darkness. Each step seemed to allow the dark to enfold the party, the light from the torches being swallowed also. A strong feeling of evil hung in every part of the caves; it was everywhere and was attaching itself to the party's very fibres. A feeling that someone or something was watching was strong too. Mutley had begun whining and held his body in a tight protective manner; Slassiantha was busying herself by looking around the cave at various rock structures. Slowly they moved on, the feeling getting stronger with each step. The cave opened into a large, open, high expanse. The rock was old and worn yet wet to look at. All over the place were stalactites hanging as thick as tree trunks, some dripping occasionally. The odd stalagmite protruded from the rough base that meandered away from them, slowly descending deeper into the ground. Kerstan held his sword aloft and continued with the torch in his other. Whispering voices could be heard, only odd words were audible so as to confuse the listener.

"Yehyess blood, I smell it," was heard suddenly in the distance.

Slassiantha stopped along with Mutley, a wind had picked up and the torches flickered. Slowly a dark shadowy mist seemed to drift in from the darkness below. The air seemed to become cold and clammy.

"I smell it I say."

All around was the feeling of people watching. Kerstan and Slassiantha held their swords aloft menacingly. Mutley had fallen to the floor and was crying openly. The mist came closer and soon seemed to reach out towards the party. The air was freezing. Voices echoed all around. A shadowy figure of a tall thin man began to appear. He was dressed in a fine silken robe and held a short staff that curled at the head. His face was smooth and was quite handsome. Smiling, he bowed sarcastically – a theatrical bow – straightening, the smile had left his face. His free left hand was held palm up and open and on it was a glowing ball of intense fire. Kerstan, Slassiantha and Mutley turned and ran deeper into the caves. He threw it in a quick fashion at the party. Kerstan dived, pushing Mutley aside, while Slassiantha jumped the other. Flames and smoke rose from the area where once they had stood. On and on into the darkness they ran. Behind they could hear an evil cackle and then all was quiet again. They did not stop as they turned the corner and plunged deeper into the stalactites that hung everywhere. After running for what felt like forever the party came to a halt, out of breath. Fearfully they looked back along the many passages they had taken, the torches began to flicker and go out so new ones were lit.

"Which way? We need to get out of here quickly." Slassiantha spoke quickly, a little too angrily. Mutley looked ready to start crying again but pointed up a slope that disappeared off to the left. The party began moving cautiously once again, listening for any sound of pursuit. The gradient seemed to be rising again which was some comfort to Kerstan, who pushed the party on faster, looking back frequently. Around the next bend the party came to a halt once again. In front was an opening with several ways leading off it. Kerstan looked at Mutley who seemed for the first time unsure. Suddenly, the feeling of cold appeared behind them again, and grabbing Slassiantha he pushed Mutley up the second passage that moved upwards at a steeper angle. All began running at a pace once again.


Arrows rained on the attackers in waves; several fell but their vast amounts meant they still came. Climbing gear was back in place and the city folk desperately fought back those that climbed before knocking the ladders down only for them to be put back up. Drarghens had flown down into the battle, their huge frames killing several horsemen at a time before being killed or sent flying off again. The city folk were outnumbered so heavily that their chances were not good, however they fought on bravely. Theorn pushed another ladder down and sent two more arrows into the creatures below yet more came still.

Blandithorpe rode hard into the crowds, swinging this way and that with his sword. Three orcs fell; turning the horse to avoid another he felt a sharp pain across his shoulder. Falling from the horse he staggered to his feet; in front of him stood a troll, its club high. The club came down hard, only reflexes saved Blandithorpe from having the club finish him. The troll had knocked him off the horse. Raising his sword, he swung to defend the next attack: club and sword connected. Blandithorpe felt as though his muscles were on fire, yet he held the sword; the troll swung again. This time Blandithorpe was unable to raise the sword again: his arms would not respond. Reflexes saved him again, an arrow shot into the rib of the troll who stopped attacking Blandithorpe. Another then another arrow hit the troll, and slowly the troll fell. Blandithorpe turned from the troll and fought other creatures near him, glancing in the direction of the arrows. Three archers were picking off creatures from a small rock foundation around twenty feet away. The fighting was everywhere: man against orc, man against troll, horseman against goblin – the fighting was intense. All creatures fought for one reason only: to destroy the city and the Source within its walls.

Upon reaching a crossroads, Slassiantha took a right, followed by the others. More noises followed. Up they went slowly, the noises gaining slowly. The same cackle could be heard. Kerstan saw a small opening and, grabbing Mutley, pushed him into it. Climbing in, he indicated that Slassiantha do the same. Slassiantha had just got in when the first passed, moving fast. Five shadowy figures, all in fine clothing. Waiting in the opening, the party listened for others. Kerstan moved out and indicated all was clear.

"Move before they return. Which way?"

Mutley looked around quickly, then pointed up a slope that drifted left. With as much speed as they could go at without making too much noise, they went. As they rose the darkness began to lighten slowly, encouraged on they moved quicker. Light from outside peeped through small cracks in the frame. Further they moved, looking back anxiously as they did. The light was stronger and the smell of fresh air was clear in the air again. Suddenly the noises began again. Behind them, so they moved on towards the light. As they turned the corner there was the exit a few hundred feet away:

it looked so beautiful, shining brightly, urging them on. Around the corner behind came the shadows. Faster they ran for the opening and as they neared out from behind a near rock came a large, ugly, horned, rubbery creature. It looked like an oversized toad with teeth. The cackle started again. Looking behind them the shadowy men watched smiling and moved slowly forward. Kerstan turned to attack but Slassiantha held him back. They were trapped between the shadows and the creature, both coming closer.

"What's keeping them?"

Kerstan's voice was a mixture of anger and frustration. Mutley had begun to cry and shook violently. Slassiantha looked from the shadows to the creature and back.

"They want us alive! They need our bodies to leave." She spoke not believing what she said; suddenly she turned and looked at the creature. A strange look crossed her face. Slassiantha ran for the creature with her sword up and ready. "This way, quickly!"

As she went the others followed; the shadow people seemed angry at the move. They rushed to stop them. Reaching the creature Slassiantha did not stop, chopping wildly she ran on, a peculiar look on her face. Her sword flashed a bright light as it hit the creature, but no resistance to it happened. Straight through the creature, Slassiantha ran outside of the caves, the light hitting her hard, her eyes burning. Kerstan and Mutley did the same before they realised what they had done.

Stumbling in the light, they fell over some rocks and rolled in the mud. Slowly they rose to their feet, rubbing their bruises, and looked around back at the caves in confusion. The cave's entrance was as black as before, nothing stirred from its opening, all was quiet. Half out of reflex, half through fear, they held their swords ready. Several seconds passed before the silence was broken by laughter. It was a weird laughter, a mixture of relief and mirth, and was coming from Slassiantha. She stood looking at the caves and just laughed. Kerstan watched her for a few seconds before he spoke.

"How? What happened back there?" He spoke in a fearful manner looking worriedly at Slassiantha.

Through laughter she spoke. "Illusions! The creature was an illusion."

Kerstan just stared at her, saying nothing for a while. "How did you know?"

"I didn't, they just stopped chasing and looked at us in desperation." Laughing again she looked from Kerstan to Mutley then back again.

Mutley was still giving both of them odd looks after they had walked for several minutes. The mist was beginning to drift away and signs of leaving the mountains started to show: vegetation began to appear again, the odd mushroom sat in small clumps at the foot of the trees. Nothing had been said by any of them for the last half hour: all walked with their own thoughts, glad to be free of the caves. Mutley seemed to be relaxing again; humming gently to himself he picked one of the mushrooms and absent-mindedly chewed at it. High in the sky, the sun was visible above the black frame yet little warmth came from its glow.

"I never want to go back in there, they were worse than the stories." As Slassiantha spoke she gave a small shiver. "What I don't understand is why they let us go."

Kerstan looked back, unconvinced they had.

Mutley, from the base of a tree where he had picked another mushroom, spoke up; his voice was sharp and startled the others.

"What you said about them needing us alive must be true." As he spoke he walked closer, offering mushrooms to them as he continued. "I don't think we would have survived otherwise, and that creature..."

He shuddered, his voice wavering towards the end of his sentence. Slassiantha put an arm around his shoulder and spoke gently. "It is all over, that creature was not real, but created to prevent us leaving."

Mutley gave a weak smile but looked back all the same.

Slowly they continued on, taking the road in a more jovial fashion, each teasing the other over trivial things to build morale again.

The mountains beyond the caves were not so dense and before long the sun was able to shine upon the party, giving better warmth to them. If the weather stayed like this then their clothes may lose the dampness by evening. Along with the vegetation, appearing slowly were the odd rodent or rabbit, not enough to make any real difference though. The party were just enjoying the walk when a sound like a small wind could be heard, then the flapping of wings. Quicker than the party had to run, the Rocs descended. Upon their backs were four bronzed women, all in fine leather armour and heavily armed with swords and axes. The Rocs were easily the size of fully-grown bull elephants and moved with such grace, landing on the ground close by the party. As soon as they touched the ground the Zinobians dismounted, their weapons ready. Kerstan was the only member of the party to have time to draw his sword, but the nearest Zinobian flipped the sword neatly out of his hand and it landed nearby in the dirt. The Zinobian women were tall, bronzed and muscular, their hair was a dark black and was tied neatly in a pigtail out of the face. All the Zinobians seemed to be beautiful, yet held an air of respect. Their weapons were of the finest quality.

Before the party had time to react, one Zinobian brought the hilt of her broadsword down onto Mutley's head; he collapsed and lay unconscious. Kerstan's reactions saved him the same fate. No harm was put upon Slassiantha. The Zinobian roughly bound Kerstan and Mutley without a word being spoken to any of them, under the guard of each other. Slassiantha watched quietly, under the same scrutiny as the others but no binding was given.

"You come see Chief." The way it was spoken was not a question.

Mutley and Kerstan were pushed hard into a net that had been laid on the ground, then two Zinobians mounted their Rocs and, pulling back on the reins, they took to the air with ease. The net jerked then roughly and took flight after the birds. Meanwhile, the other two had pushed Slassiantha onto one Roc and one Zinobian had mounted behind her. The other mounted the other and they flew to join the others. The flight was smooth and took only a few minutes. Slassiantha held on tightly, watching the birds in front that shook the net mercilessly about as they flew. Suddenly the Rocs descended upon their village.

The village was primitive and consisted of stick huts with thatched roofs and some fencing placed around the perimeter. Chicken and cattle roamed the area freely; Zinobian women were going about their duties. Some were flying Rocs and shooting arrows at small bags, each shot as accurate as the next. Others practised fighting each other; such speed and determination was put into everything they did. Armour was being made and even children as young as five were practising. A fire burned in the centre and had a large black pot standing on it. Men were attending the pot.

Landing, Slassiantha was made to dismount and then the Zinobian dismounted gracefully as well. The two carrying the net flew on another few steps then the net was dropped from the height into a large pit.

The journey had been most uncomfortable for Kerstan, bound and unable to help himself. Mutley lay unconscious on top of him on several occasions. Kerstan looked around, trying to take in the route that they had taken. Suddenly the Rocs had descended and the net had flown at quite a pace over a village then been released and dropped into a pit. Landing with a thud, the wind had been knocked out of Kerstan; Mutley had stirred yet still lay unconscious. With great difficulty, Kerstan righted himself then worked on releasing his hands. Slassiantha was out there and needed him.

The men in the camp kept their heads low and, avoiding any attention, looked after the young or cooked. Slassiantha had watched in curiosity until rudely stopped. Two Zinobian were approaching the landing crew and the Zinobian nearest nudged her to look toward them. Slassiantha ignored the approaching women and stared towards the pit.

"What is going to happen to them?"

Slassiantha spat out the words with such venom the Zinobian seemed surprised. The Zinobian ignored her and turned her to face the approaching Zinobian. Slassiantha crossly turned back and asked again, this time in a more gentle fashion. The answer came quickly and in a matter of fact way.

"Food. We need to eat."

Slassiantha was about to answer back, but the two arrived and spoke over her, demanding that she be taken to the Chief. Without further time being wasted, the Zinobian marched Slassiantha off protesting towards a large hut near the centre of the camp. Slassiantha found herself studying the two Zinobians that had approached; both were older, that was clear enough to see, but both had the same beauty about them. It took a short while to cross to the hut, upon arriving the elder Zinobian entered with a deep bow. Slassiantha stood with the two younger women and waited impatiently, taking the opportunity to watch the others training. Slassiantha was amazed at the skill and accuracy of even the young until she thought of their dedication to any task.

The hut door stirred and the elder Zinobian appeared.

"Enter. Greatbird will see you." The tone was not to be considered but demanding. Slassiantha was not given time to consider and was pushed through the door into the hut.

The inside was well lit with torches that hung from the walls. It was finely furnished with a wooden table and chairs, a black framed bed made of closely packed straw, and a structure that held some leather armour and an axe, both of the highest quality. Sitting on one of the chairs, pushed to the edge of the room, was the little girl she had seen on the Roc: once helplessly fighting to survive the attack from the Clickers and now calm. Her face held a stern, tight-lipped look. Standing in a robe of a wolf skin tied tightly with a thick cord was the Chief. Greatbird was a woman of around five feet tall, yet her body was covered with enormous muscles, bronzed and just as beautiful as the next. She held herself in a powerful way and demanded respect from all who she honoured with her presence.

"You show how create fiery demon."

The way she spoke and moved did not give the option to consider the question, however Slassiantha stood her ground angrily. Squaring up to Greatbird, she gave a look of annoyance before answering.

"You release my companions then we talk."

Slassiantha staggered under the slap that was given to her face by one of the elder Zinobians. Righting herself she gave a stern look at the Zinobian before returning her look to the Chief. Waiting, she sucked her sore lip but her eyes never left the Chief at all. The Chief looked Slassiantha up and down then spoke again.

"Show us NOW."

Slassiantha stood up straight and taking a deep breath spoke once again, this time in a pleading fashion. "Please release them, they need to be going. Then I teach."

Surprise crossed the Chief's face. "You are weak, what need are they?"

Slassiantha tried to control her anger but the words came out of her mouth with a force. "They must find a Catcher or the city and all will be destroyed."

Several seconds passed before the Chief nodded. One of the elder Zinobian left the hut, returning later with Kerstan holding a semi-conscious Mutley around the shoulder. Kerstan watched all the Zinobians warily, but seemed calm.

"Teach us." Greatbird spoke with a little anger this time.

Slassiantha looked at Kerstan and Mutley then slowly back at the Chief. Speaking in an authoritative way, she gave a look of menace.

"I will when you show respect to my wishes."

The Zinobian nearest her raised her hand again; this time Slassiantha was ready and raised her own. The Zinobian left the floor with such a force and flew into the opposite wall it was like no one had touched her. Slowly, she shook herself and stood again. The others went to attack but the Chief clapped and all was still. Slassiantha gave a look of such furiousness that the Chief just stood there watching.

"They go, you teach?"

This time the last was a question.

"Yes, they go, I teach."

Kerstan went to argue but the stern look given stopped him.

Slassiantha agreed on the condition that they left unharmed and with weapons. The Chief agreed and a couple of the finest swords were brought in. Kerstan sheathed his then took the other and tied it to his back; carefully he guided Mutley out of the hut and cautiously out of the camp. The Miredith Mountains could be seen from the camp, a good three hours' journey away. As Kerstan moved off, Mutley stirred a little on his shoulder. Being a distance from the camp, he placed him on the ground and washed his face with water from his backpack. Mutley opened his eyes and looked around slowly, blinked a few times, then smiled.

"So we escaped did we. Where's Slassiantha?"

The Zinobian women watched them go and waited till they had put a reasonable distance between them before the two young Zinobians followed. The Chief had suggested it may be good to keep them alive if the teaching was to continue, but unless necessary they were not to know. The Chief had agreed after the look that Slassiantha had given.

Slassiantha took a deep breath and let it out slowly as she surveyed her prison for the next day or so. For prison is what it felt like. Slassiantha knew that Kerstan and Mutley would be dead if not for her and that she had to teach to keep them that way. The Catchers had to be found or all would suffer. Although primitive in essence, the people had a real sense of pride and enthusiasm in all they did. Perhaps staying could be interesting? Her thoughts were broken by a voice; turning she saw the Chief was approaching her slowly. Greatbird outside in the open was much more formidable, her skin taut with sinew and muscle. A small smile that had been on the Chief's face left her as she focused on Slassiantha.

"You teach me and my guards only."

Her voice was one of authority yet had a calm about it.

Slassiantha smiled and looked at the mixed women standing nearby. All were beautiful as all Zinobian seemed to be and all held themselves straight and importantly. Clothed in fine leather and armed with swords or axes sheathed at their sides, they all eyed Slassiantha with an uncertain look. Slassiantha smiled again, this time at the guards, then turned her attention to the task ahead.

"All can learn magic, not all will be effective."

Blandithorpe had remounted a horse and, giving a great yell, had steered it deep into the orcs again. The orcs stood hard and only a few fell. The battle was now everywhere and smoke filled the sky from small fires started. The sky was red with an angry look to it. Rain came now in heavy barrages that soaked through to the skin in seconds, the floor was a slippery mass of mud and mire. Buckenbear was using his axe with such skill that creatures fell like flies. The city folk were fighting hard and so far had protected the city from capture. Inside the chapel, Xendon had joined the Zenithe and used his magic to try to strengthen the Zenithe as they poured more and more power into the Source. The Source glowed brightly but began to show sign of slowing. Zenithe lay exhausted and drained, everywhere they lay they were replaced by others, the demand was so great. The battle outside had put great pressure on the Source, but the city folk seemed to be winning. The creatures began to look like they were being beaten; slowly they retreated from the walls. The creatures turned and ran, many being cut down in the retreat. Tired from the battle, Blandithorpe had taken a nasty blow from a troll. He had been thrown from his horse and died before hitting the floor. With the creatures in retreat, Alanthos turned his horse and called the men to return to the safety of the gates; it would not be long before they returned. Once safely through the gates Alanthos collapsed from his horse, exhausted and unable to stay in the saddle any longer. Several men caught him and took him off to feed and rest.

"Who's in charge here?"

The voice came from Buckenbear, who studied the people milling around. Theorn came over from the battlements and, taking his hand, shook it heartedly.

"We will want paying well for this."

Buckenbear smiled openly before clapping Theorn hard on the back and strolling off to find food. Theorn and Buckenbear had just about finished their food when the sentry's horn blew again.

"Creatures approaching fast again, back to your mounts," Theorn yelled.

Men rose to join those already defending; Theorn ran to climb the stairs to the tower to look at the approaching enemy. He had virtually finished the climb when he saw Alanthos already looking over the wall. Alanthos had a look of utter despair on his face and was talking to the sentries; Xendon was on the tower too. The whole demeanour of him was in tatters, his face was drawn and tired and seemed to have aged considerably. Theorn looked out at the oncoming enemy and was taken by surprise at what he saw. The mass of creatures was bigger than before and was coming at a pace;

the city folk that were ready to defend were fewer and tired. This time would be harder for all concerned. The only consolation was a break in the rain, however the black clouds loomed in the distance and had an eerie red glow to them.

Kerstan and Mutley had both trudged on for the last hour in silence. Kerstan was deep in thought over the loss of a travelling partner and Mutley was tracking a set of tracks that he thought could be of interest. The mountains had been successfully left behind them and the mist was diminishing gradually so the tracking had become easier. The sun had come out completely and this time had its strength back. The few bushes that appeared, darted among the dry grass and prickly thorns, had some berries on, and other small plants could be seen in odd patches. So far no other animal or human had been seen but the tracks may prove favourable.

"We may eat a proper meal tonight."

Mutley spoke in a more cheerful fashion and smiled towards Kerstan before re-checking the tracks. Mirintirith was not too far off and this managed to spur them on at a quicker pace. Their hopes were filled with finding the Catchers and that the journey may well soon be over. A rabbit dashed across their path and disappeared as quickly, Mutley missing it with a stone from his sling. It took Kerstan only a few minutes to trap the rabbit and then kill it, returning with a grin of triumph on his face.

"Dinner is served."

Mutley began gathering other roots and vegetation from around, along with sticks for a fire. They would eat well tonight. Then, refreshed, they could enter Mirintirith ready to search again. Mirintirith was a land full of rich vegetation and fresh running streams so would provide many good meals till the Catchers were found. A good place for any creature to live. Also the last place where Catchers had been seen. With enough to create a fire and a good meal they stopped and set up camp. Soon a small fire was going, the first decent meal cooking on it as well.

The Zinobian men continued to clean and cook all the time, avoiding any eye contact whatsoever from the women. Especially the new visitor. Slassiantha sat watching the five guards and Greatbird from a distance, her arms crossed in a lazy fashion under her breasts. After a short explanation they were attempting their first magic, a simple spell to make a stone glow a faint golden orangey colour. A wry smile slid over her face as she watched; the guards were all concentrating hard with various degree of success. Each guard and Greatbird had sweat on their faces and stared in wonder at the rocks. Most sat there with no effect at all but two had a slight glow to them. Sitting watching from her perch on a hay bale nearby was the little girl that had been on the Roc; her face was one of mixed emotions and she sat as if ready to leap on an approaching prey; her eyes hung out on stalks. A small dribble was running unnoticed down her chin as she watched. Slassiantha had seen her but was trying to ignore her. Slassiantha had found out that the little girl was the Chief's daughter and the informant for her capture.

"You must keep concentration or the glow will stop."

Two Zinobian guards were getting quite excited at their achievements, however the Chief did not look too pleased as her attempt had failed. As the guards struggled to create or maintain the glow, Greatbird turned and spoke harshly at Slassiantha.

"Teach us something new," she growled.

Slassiantha gave a look that a mother would give an awkward child and spoke in an authoritative manner.

"No. You must master one before moving on or you may harm yourself or others."

Greatbird seemed to straighten herself and her face took on a disgusted look. "Teach or die!"

Slassiantha stared at Greatbird, giving her a long and hard stare. After some time she nodded and answered.

"Have it your way. Let's try blocking a passage."

Slassiantha stood up from the rock slowly and signalled to the guards to stop and listen. Slowly and deliberately, Slassiantha scoured the ground until a small rock of around her fist size was found. Holding the rock she tossed it high into the air; the rock spun then dipped back towards earth at a pace. As the rock dropped Slassiantha raised her hand and the rock slowed then stopped in a quick pace, then Slassiantha made a flick of her wrist and the rock spun off towards her indicated direction to land some feet away in the dust. Throughout the demonstration Slassiantha had given a running commentary and finished by staring towards Greatbird for her approval. Greatbird was not slow in giving her approval so Slassiantha went slowly through the whole spell again.

"Now, find a stone not too big and practise both spells on the stone." Slassiantha stopped one guard as she went to pick up a stone. "This spell takes stamina so start small."

Greatbird was waiting for another Zinobian to have a go first, so one guard a little reluctantly did. The stone had been thrown high and was arcing back down when the woman began her attempt. The stone was not much bigger than a golf ball and made a small change in direction then arced abruptly; seeing its flight she tried to correct it and failed.

The stone came down at a pace and hit another guard across the shoulder blade; the crack was sharp and the guard winced in pain. Although in pain the guard made to lunge at the other, but Slassiantha was quick to react. Both guards stopped abruptly in mid stride, bouncing off an invisible wall. Slowly they both rose to their feet.

"This spell needs time and stamina." Slassiantha spoke again, directing the words harshly at Greatbird. "Let us return to the firefly spell."

Greatbird was about to argue when Slassiantha gave her a look that stopped her. Training returned to the first spell with new vigour. While the guards continued Slassiantha found her interest swayed to watch other Zinobians fighting; their skill was better than any she had seen before. Slassiantha caught the eye of the little girl and forced herself to return to watching the guards. By evening all had accomplished the firefly and three were blocking a passage, one an older guard on a stone much the same size as Slassiantha. Slassiantha left the training tired yet pleased with the progress made. The older Zinobian (Ikdriss) had a kinder attitude towards Slassiantha and walked with her back towards the Chief's hut.

"We leave to hunt for food, you rest a while." She gave a warm smile.

To Slassiantha's surprise she found herself asking if she could go along too. It was agreed and the elder Zinobian and two younger ones joined Slassiantha. The Zinobians moved with ease and blended easily with their surroundings. A younger Zinobian held back with Slassiantha so as not to attract attention. They had been out for around ten minutes when they came across a small party of lizard men. From their advantage point they made their attack, smooth, quick, and effective. The attack had been a success, the lizard men having not been able to resist the attack as well as if prepared.

However, one Zinobian, the other younger one, had taken a severe bite to her thigh. The wound was deep and the lizard's poisonous saliva had taken effect badly. Bleeding and in much pain, she lay on the floor. Slassiantha put her sword away and took her backpack off, digging deep into the bag for her medical kit that she had used as a nurse in the great battles. While she did this, the elder Zinobian drew an arrow and shot it quickly and precisely between her eyes. The injured Zinobian died instantly and the elder lent over to close the eyes of the younger. Without any sign of remorse, she lifted the dead Zinobian and helped lift the lizard men onto the shoulders of the other Zinobian women, then headed home back to the camp. It took Slassiantha several seconds to put her backpack back on and follow from a distance. Slassiantha was struggling to come to terms with what she had seen, was it real, had she really seen one Zinobian kill another? She could have helped, surely she could have. The journey back was a long one as far as Slassiantha felt, all the way she puzzled over the attack. By the time she had arrived at the camp she was sure that to stay was too dangerous. When escape was possible she would leave.

Following the Zinobian to where they put the dead, she then turned and half in a daze walked to sit quietly outside the Chief's. Sitting watching, she saw Zinobians practising sword fighting. Others were practising archery, some from Rocs' backs, still as accurate as on foot. Still others made various pieces of armour or weapons, all of finery beyond most she had seen in the city. The men were cooking the meal, avoiding all attention; this only added to her fear. The sentries, some the Chief's guard, were everywhere. The guards were practising the spells with some confidence. How was she going to escape? But escape she would.

The smell of cooking broke her thoughts. She turned her attention to two men turning a spit, two figures undistinguishable. Whatever it was, it smelt lovely. Other men were cutting and preparing odd-looking vegetables. Their fear of acknowledgment was great, especially from the Chief. Relaxing a little, Slassiantha watched all in silence. Dinner was not long to wait for. Soon the men were preparing the eating area. When the meal was ready the men indicated and the Zinobians stopped their various tasks. All sat but the men, who cowered at a distance ready to serve the food when ready. The guards ate first, then once the Chief seemed satisfied, all the others did. Once the Zinobian women had had their fill, the men ate the leftovers. The meal had tasted as good as it had smelt. The meat was tender and not too strong; the vegetables were delicious. Slassiantha had not realised just how hungry she had been but found that she had eaten two large plates and was on her third.

Darkness was drawing in so Slassiantha made her way back to the Chief's hut to prepare her bed in the hay. Greatbird was already back and so was the Chief's daughter. The camp was becoming quiet except for the odd moo from the cattle or the sound of the sentries walking around the camp. Slassiantha made her excuses and went to bed; lying on the hay she waited for the opportunity to escape. It had turned late when Slassiantha was certain her fellow occupants were asleep. Rising as quietly and slowly as she could, she made her way to the entrance of the hut. Looking out, the camp was still all except for the occasional sentry. Slassiantha waited until a chicken fighting another for the scraps left from dinner distracted the closest sentry. Looking back to check, Greatbird and the girl slept she slipped outside. Slassiantha was about to slip away when a young voice spoke to her.

"Can't you sleep? What's wrong?"

Turning quickly, Slassiantha saw the young girl poking her head out of the hut, rubbing sleep from her eyes. Her face was one of concern, not suspicion. Slassiantha put a finger to her mouth and whispered.

"I couldn't sleep so was trying to clear my head, that is all."

Slassiantha had not felt she had sounded too convincing yet smiled anyway.

"What's wrong?" the little girl asked again. Her voice was beginning to show signs of suspicion. Slassiantha spoke again in a whisper.

"Nothing for you to worry about, something I saw while hunting."

The little girl looked puzzled but answered, "Tell me, I may be able to help."

As Slassiantha considered her options the little girl turned to re-enter the hut. "I will wake Mum and you can tell her, if you prefer."

The little girl's face took on a look of distrust. Slassiantha quickly grabbed the girl by the arm, pulling her free from the entrance.

"No don't! Out hunting I saw one of your tribe killed."

The little girl gave a screwed up look before replying, "So she died, Zinobians can die."

Slassiantha squirmed awkwardly yet had no choice but to continue. "She was killed by one of her own!"

The little girl listened then began to smile a knowing look. "She was hurt badly, wasn't she?"

Slassiantha agreed but still did not understand so the girl continued.

"In our culture if one of us will slow or hinder it is better to die, in fact an honour to die."

Slassiantha listened to the girl and a look of utter disgust crossed her face.

"It is an honour to kill the inflicted."

The girl spoke with sincere pride. Slassiantha turned on the girl in anger.

"I could have helped her."

The girl's reaction was one of mixed anger and sympathy. "We lack the resources to help, they are so scarce."

Her speech indicated a resignation to the problem yet real sorrow. Slassiantha still had one question unanswered that needed answering. She did not want to ask but had to.

"Did we... I eat your fellow woman today?"

As the girl answered she looked for the first time uncomfortable and upset. "Yes, we need to eat. It is an honour."

Slassiantha felt guilt at asking and took the girl in her arms to comfort her. Fighting back tears, the girl pushed Slassiantha away angrily.

"Don't, I am a warrior not a baby!"

Slassiantha moved away apologetically and after a few seconds asked the girl her name. The girl gave her a quizzical look but answered, "They call me Morning Dew."

The girl seemed to relax as she spoke and a small smile crept over her face. "Can I ask you a question?"

Slassiantha seemed surprised at the girl but nodded to continue. The girl took a deep breath, steadied herself unconsciously, then continued. "I can make a stone glow brightly but moving it, how do you do that again?"

The girls face had lit up in anticipation. Slassiantha stared open-mouthed at Morning Dew as she spoke.

"You are performing magic without appropriate training." As she spoke the words hit her. Morning Dew was doing magic at her age! And she was untrained. "How did you manage it?"

Morning Dew stood up straight with pride. Smiling widely she answered, "Magic comes naturally to me!" The little girl studied Slassiantha's face before continuing. "Can you teach me more?"

Slassiantha was still trying to accept the facts but agreed to teach Morning Dew. However, she asked that her mother was not told and it was done in secret.

"You are too young to learn by teaching standards."

Slassiantha smiled in a reassured manner at Morning Dew then spoke quietly again. "Tell me, you say magic comes naturally. Can you explain?"

Morning Dew smiled back then drew up a small bale of straw that had been nearby for cattle to feed off and indicated that they sat. Once settled, she began to talk about what she had accomplished. "When I was young I found that if I concentrated plants grew berries..."

The clouds had a fierce red about them and the wind had picked up, throwing the heavy rain at the hard rock wall of the city. Sitting high in one of the watchtowers were Alanthos and Xendon. They had climbed the tower to talk freely of their worries and fears without others overhearing. Xendon still had not forgiven himself for the damage done to the gate and had spoke of his concerns of it happening again. Looking out into the ever-increasing bad weather, they looked at the multitude of creatures that battled everywhere; their numbers had grown over the hours.

"Where are Tinden and Shadma? What's taking them so long?"

Xendon had spoken out in frustration, not expecting an answer; Alanthos gave the answer anyway.

"It will take time to persuade the giants if ever, you know they distrust humans. The fact that Shadma is one of them may help."

Their attention was forced back to the ongoing battle, its cries covering their conversation. Trolls had managed to retake an area and were reassembling the catapults; horsemen fought wildly around them to stop the progress. Orcs and goblins were everywhere; the city folk seemed to be outnumbered badly yet they still held off the inevitable. Lightning lit another tower and Xendon saw Theorn chopping at a climbing gear and the climbers falling. The sky was getting darker as evening approached: soon visibility would become so low that the enemy could possibly gain access without being noticed.

Alanthos clapped Xendon on the back, gave a quick smile, then left at a pace down the stairs to regroup an army of horsemen. Leaning over the wall, Xendon threw bolts of fire from his staff into the fray. Soon a small group of thirty horsemen and twenty archers had been gathered. Alanthos gave the signal and the massive bar of the gates was removed. The gates opened and instantly the horsemen drove their horses out at a gallop, the following archers having given a volley of arrows to clear the way for them. The gates were shut again and the bar replaced. The archers had soon taken positions and were picking out their targets from their hiding places amongst the various rocks around the base of the battlements; some extra lay there provided by catapults. Alanthos rode his horse wildly into the mass of creatures. His fellow horsemen did the same; the battle had taken another level.


Shadma shook his head. His vision was blurred and his temples ached. The heavy bruising was beginning to hinder vision and speech. Shadma spoke between the next beatings.

"It is true Snode has gathered an army that threatens to destroy..."

His voice had taken on a desperate tone and was cut off by a sharp blow to the jaw. For the last hour Shadma had shared a space in the street of the town along with Tinden. Both hung between two posts, attached heavily by chains around their arms, legs spreadeagle. The giants, upon being told to find out the real reason for their visit, had taken the opportunity to give them both a beating. Tinden's small frame had taken all it could and hung limp and awkwardly lifeless, with little unmarked flesh showing. One giant around twelve feet in height hit Shadma again. With all his strength the vine held in his hand whipped across the thigh of Shadma; a cruel, satisfied smile crept over the giant's face.

"You lie, human-lover." The words curled his mouth in disgust and were said with real venom. "No troll, however stupid they are, would leave their caves and battle for anything, especially a city."

His cruel face screwed up in enjoyment as he swung again.

"Enough, get them down. I'll get to the facts."

His fun had been stopped by the approach of Maxinton. Shadma rolled his body as tight as the chains would allow and gave a pleading look towards Maxinton.

"You must listen, I tell the truth and time is running out!"

Cutting the chains loose, Shadma and Tinden's frames hit the floor mercilessly and then curled up in agony. Tinden showed little signs of life. As Maxinton spoke again his tone had changed to one of annoyance and expecting to be listened to.

"Why should we, human-lover?"

The words rolled off his tongue with a spiteful edge. Shadma lay there on the floor and looked at the giant. It had been many years since he had last seen Maxinton and he had gained some weight. Even with the extra weight he was a formidable character. Shadma had left the camp several years ago in search of his fortune after tales of magic and battles. When he had left he had been made fun of and had caused embarrassment to his family and his cousin, as he was meant to join the giants of the guard. He knew he had humiliated his cousin yet he had had to go as he had been tired of his life and longed for adventure. Now his cousin stood before him and was going to pay him back for his humiliation. Shadma tried another approach.

"Maxinton, cousin, you have to listen! I tell the truth."

Maxinton straightened his huge frame and gave a deep smile. "I don't have to do anything!"

The next Shadma knew all was going black and his head hurt from a swift kick from Maxinton.

As Kerstan and Mutley ate their meal their thoughts were on the city and on Slassiantha. Kerstan had concerns for her as he knew little of the tribe and what he knew was not complimentary. Chewing absent-mindedly on a piece of root, he suddenly felt a strange feeling. He felt a mixture of excitement and fear; looking around he could not see any reason for his last. Turning his thoughts back to the root, he chewed on it, losing interest as he did. The feeling returned yet stronger, and with it the feeling of being watched. Abruptly he stood, looking around as he did. Mutley gave a yell and fell over backwards.

As Kerstan looked around he saw off in the distance a small burgundy creature. The creature was looking at him also, but then disappeared back into the undergrowth. The feeling went just as quickly. Yet in his mind he sensed that the creature had been real and was going to return. Kerstan's mind was in turmoil – was the story told by Slassiantha real? Was Catcher blood in his veins? How could he sense the thoughts of the creature?

Mutley was on his feet and looking in the direction in fear. The fire and meal had been forgotten. Mutley kicked the fire out and took his sword uneasily in his hand. Kerstan put his hand on Mutley's and shook his head, indicating to re-sheath the weapon. Mutley did so grudgingly. Slowly both made their way in the direction of the creatures last seen position. Kerstan tried to listen to his feelings again. He could sense that the creature was not alone and was watching, yet wherever he looked there was no creature.

"Please come out, we will not hurt you."

Kerstan felt the distrust and waited patiently; Mutley went to speak and Kerstan stopped him. No movement was made by anything. Suddenly Kerstan felt various emotions: distrust, fear, then anger. All had happened over a short period. He could not understand the feelings yet he sensed them.

"Come out please, we will not hurt you."

Kerstan spoke again, this time in an urgent fashion. Suddenly a noise was heard from behind him; spinning both had their swords out instinctively. Two young Zinobians stood there and in their arms was a furious creature. Its body was puffed up and its tongue shot in and out in an angry fashion. Kerstan moved quickly towards the Zinobians.

"Don't hurt him, let him go. I need to talk to him."

The Zinobians looked at Kerstan, at his sword, then in disbelief did as requested. Upon release, the Catcher looked from Zinobian to Kerstan then vanished. The Zinobians moved to follow but were stopped by Kerstan. Kerstan could still sense the Catcher was near. Angrily Kerstan turned on the Zinobians.

"What do you think you are doing? We need their help, not to frighten them away!"

Kerstan was furious and was ready to use the sword in his hand. The Zinobians just looked at him in confusion, yet made no move to defend.

From behind some bushes a few feet away two Catchers appeared; their keen yellow eyes studied the others closely. Slowly and very guardedly the Catchers approached.

"Who are you?"

The squeaky voice of the Catcher had a tinge of fear yet recognition about it; both stood at a distance and watched closely. Kerstan was taken by surprise by the squeaky voice. For several long seconds he stood and stared at the Catchers. Mutley and the Zinobians did the same. The next time the Catcher spoke it was only a small distance from the party. Its burgundy body was visibly breathing fast and tense. The other, an older Catcher, just stood and seemed to be ready to attack if needed.

"Who are you? I sense I know you, but how?"

Kerstan uneasily answered, his voice was tense and quivered slightly. "What? How can I know you, yet I feel I do too!"

The words had left his mouth before he realised and Kerstan felt foolish having said them. Mutley and the Zinobians watched in silence, now from a short distance.

"Who are you?"

The Catcher spoke this time in anger and ruffled his spikes, ready to attack. Realising his lack of response Kerstan answered. "Sorry, I'm Kerstan Wholphsan."

Both Catchers looked over Kerstan like a man buying a vessel. Slowly recognition appeared upon their faces. With an odd smile the younger spoke again.

"I believe that you are, I sense it. Legend says that half-Catcher half-man would come, how is this so?"

Both the Catchers' keen yellow eyes were fixed upon Kerstan, seemingly unaware of the others. Both waited for his answer.

"I am not sure but I can guess." Unsure of how best to continue, Kerstan took a deep breath, rubbed his chin, then continued. "A friend believed and told me that I was given blood from a Catcher."

Both Catchers were completely silent as he spoke.

"I have no recollection of this but I guess that would make me half-man half-Catcher." Kerstan studied their reactions then continued, the words coming easier. "I was working with Dr Hanston, his wife, and daughter, Slassiantha, the one who told me. I was burnt badly by fire and needed blood, so I was told."

The Catchers listened then seemed to consider, then simply turned and vanished. The party stood there dazed and unsure of their next move. It was Mutley who broke the silence, spitting out the words at Kerstan.

"How long were you going to keep that secret?"

Kerstan looked across and shrugged his shoulders; it didn't matter now the Catchers had left. Why and would they return?


It was dark and Shadma woke to severe pain from his ribs. Rolling slowly onto his front, he groaned as he pushed himself into a sitting position. Slowly his eyes adjusted to the dark around him. The only light came through the cracks in the stick walls of the cellar in which he had been placed. Over on some hay lay Tinden in a tight ball, covered with deep gashes and blood that had started to scab. Tinden lay in a helpless state and breathed in a low rasping fashion. Why had he asked him to come along with him? He had known it would be dangerous yet was glad for the company. His own body, upon examination, was in a bad way also; his cousin seemed to enjoy the punishment that he had given out. Sitting up straight again Shadma winced as he considered his options. Tinden moaned and moved slightly, his breathing increased slightly before he lay still again. Shadma looked across at his helpless body and sighed deeply.

"Sorry, you never deserved this."

A key in a lock broke the quiet and suddenly blinding light coming from the doorway broke the darkness. Coming down the wooden stairs was Maxinton, upon his face was a look of mixed emotions.

"I've checked your statement and there seems to be some truth to it."

Shadma stirred slightly and Maxinton snapped out the next. "That doesn't change how I feel about everything."

Shadma sneered at Maxinton and spoke in a quiet reserve. "Good for you, I thought we were friends!"

Ignoring Maxinton he turned his attention to Tinden. Slowly he forced his aching body to where Tinden lay. Upon reaching him he began bathing his wounds from a bucket of water left for them to drink from. Tinden, upon close examination, was in a worse state than first thought. The gashes were deep welts and the blood was still fresh and dripped occasionally. Tenderly he began to wash the wounds. Maxinton was watching as Shadma tended to Tinden. Shadma really did seem to care about this funny-looking twig man. Something that he found hard to accept. The culture of giants was to look after their own and keep themselves to themselves. Shadma continued to ignore Maxinton and began gently washing the blood away. Maxinton moved awkwardly to join Shadma in caring for Tinden. Taking the ladle from the bucket he poured some water over the area Shadma was tending to. Shadma gave a quick glance at Maxinton and smiled, then returned to the task ahead.


The Catchers had left at quite a pace; their thoughts were a mixture of intrigue and anguish. Having run for a short while they stopped and slowed, out of the sight of the party. Taking a cutting into some tall reed-like plants, they headed on a short distance more to join the other Catchers. Three other Catchers were waiting and had been wondering if the legend was true. Their waiting came to an abrupt end when the two Catchers rushed up. The younger spoke in an excited fashion.

"He is the one the legend talks of, Kerstan has come!"

A short, elderly Catcher that had considerable years on the others spoke in an angry fashion.

"He is human, he is dangerous." As he spoke he raised his battle-scarred body high in a powerful display of authority. "Yes, humans are not to be trusted."

The youngster was keen to enter into the conversation but the look given shut him up. An oversized Catcher that lolled around wheezing spoke up next.

"If he is the one all will be alright."

The older Catcher was pacing by now and thrashed about his body, moving nimbly for his age. "NO! He is human and is dangerous."

"But if…"

The oversized Catchers words were cut short. The young Catcher spoke with anxiety, his voice raised.

"We must listen then decide. He is Kerstan."


As Alanthos spurred on his horse the rain hammered down; it had such a force to it that it stung his face. Through clenched teeth he rode, his vision impaired, chopping orcs and goblin wherever they stood. Swinging his heavy sword with fervour much like that of his younger days, he scattered the creatures. Blow after blow they fell; soon he was deep in the battle. Other horsemen were with him; their weapons helping in the destruction of the creatures. The sky was a heavy shade of red and had an eerie presence about it. The various creatures easily outnumbered them yet they fought on bravely with amazing confidence. The Source was beginning to crumble and bits decaying fell off to the floor. Some Zenithe lay exhausted while others worked on in desperation.

As Alanthos turned his horse he was thrown from its saddle. On his feet now, he continued to fight. Only his great skill kept the creatures at a distance. Thankful for a volley of arrows, he carried on. Tiring and needing a break he retreated, taking cover from the now near archers as they continued to send volley after volley into the battle. Still the creatures came. Theorn prepared the battlements for an inevitable attack, commanding the troops around him with authority from many a battle. Xendon had filled small pots with the sap of the incopedian and was catapulting the substance into the mass of creatures with devastating power. Orcs, trolls and goblins fell in large quantities as holes appeared in the ground around them; confusion helped to delay the attack on the gates. As more troops joined the battle, Alanthos retreated to take a rest. His body was aching and showing signs of age, much to his annoyance.

The Source shone in brilliance, its power to protect called upon like never in a long time. Decaying under the pressure it continued to give sacrificially, the Zenithe doing all they could to restore the power to keep the Source alive. The atmosphere was one of frustration and anger, yet they diligently continued. The battle was in full swing as Snode rode over the crest of a hill to gaze upon the battle against the city.

With evil eyes he surveyed his armies; puffing out his grotesque body he smiled a wicked smile. His tail swished menacingly from his position on his horse. Hand on the reins, he barked commands to all who listened. A huge mace hung on the saddle and in his hand was his staff, the bramble glowing an evil red. Snode raised his body high in the saddle and with a mighty yell sent his Sleepers to join the battle. Four creatures – a mixture of a wild-cat and a spider – sped off eagerly into the fray. Teeth gnashing at all in their way, they scattered the creatures. With incredible speed they set off towards the gates.


The hard work and tender care shown Tinden was beginning to show results. Tinden, although still extremely sore, sat on the hay and helped to bathe and strap the various welts, a weary smile across his face. Maxinton had an unusual smile on his face as he helped, and seemed to be enjoying the feeling of helping. Shadma clapped a huge arm around his shoulder and smiled back before continuing in wrapping Tinden's wounds. Through swollen lips a shallow and rasping voice came from Tinden as he propped himself back up on the hay once again.

"Thank you Maxinton, it is very appreciated."

Shadma, with gentleness unnatural for such a huge frame, helped Tinden to his feet and then gave him some water to drink. Tinden swayed slightly then righted himself before sitting down on a small sack of oats.

"Please reconsider helping, we do need help."

Shadma had spoken quietly and almost apologetically yet he had spoken. Maxinton, through eyes that seemed less defiant, looked upon both of his captives. Confusion was set deep in his face.

"Why do you care so deeply for others? It is not natural."

The statement was not meant to offend but was a genuine question. Shadma smiled and placed his hand gently on his cousin's as he spoke.

"They help us when we need help, they are the same really."

Maxinton seemed to be considering the answer but shook his head regretfully anyway. "They are not the same, they care, we tolerate. There is a difference."

The words seemed to sting as Maxinton spoke them and his face screwed up a little. Feeling ashamed Maxinton looked away.

Tinden placed his twiggy hand on the knee of Maxinton; it looked like a doll's hand in comparison.

"You have shown that you care, please show again and help."

As Tinden spoke he tried to hug Maxinton, only managing to hold a small part of his frame. Maxinton had turmoil all over his face and for several seconds sat heavily on the floor in silence.

"I will talk to the Chief. That is all I can do."

The words were said with a lot of sympathy. Shadma smiled at Maxinton and giving him a warm pat on the back replied, "That is enough. Thank you."

Mutley was still muttering to himself as he repacked his backpack in silence for the third time. Kerstan had said nothing since the Catchers had disappeared and that had been several minutes ago. The Zinobians had searched the area to no avail and had returned a little embarrassed by their failure. Kerstan was fed up with himself: he had come this far, had seen a Catcher, then foolishly allowed it to escape again. Although he had believed that he did the will of the Source, they had left! Kerstan could still feel their presence and was sure they were watching, but they had not returned. With reluctance he picked up his pack and gave one last check around. A good four hundred yards away stood four burgundy figures half hidden by the reed-like bushes and they were watching cautiously. Kerstan indicated to the others and then all stood still and watched. Slowly the Catchers approached.

Slassiantha had woken early and been out hunting with the women before training had begun. Training was going well and Slassiantha was feeling a sense of pride in the extent to which the guards had accomplished the tasks presented them. All had accomplished making stones glow and most could change the direction they travelled in mid-air. One guard, a shorter woman yet no less formidable, had really managed to master this spell and could direct the stones with some accuracy. She had taken to bouncing them off chickens' heads, much to the amusement of the others, all except Greatbird who had given her a look that stopped her quicker than any arrow could. Although the lessons were hard and took both concentration and stamina, the interest had grown. The other Zinobians had begun to watch but so far had not been given permission to join in the training. Morning Dew had risen early and sat in her usual area, taking a fine interest in the training. In the evening when she and Slassiantha could slip away, her training had taken place. Training had gone well, in fact was going so well that she had advanced to creating little bunny-like creatures that soon faded. Slassiantha was still determined to keep the training quiet, much to the annoyance of

Morning Dew.

"That is much better, mind the chickens."

Slassiantha was getting quite fond of the quaint tribal women and was enjoying their company as she trained. She had come to terms with some of their more undesirable actions as necessary. They needed to survive and survive they did well. Their fighting skills left hardened fighters standing and their hunting skills were not far off either. Slassiantha, having joined them in hunting, had felt it had been both enlightening and a pleasure.

"One more time then we may try creating a small animal."

The Zinobians seemed to jump at the chance and several stones flew enthusiastically in all directions. The chickens ran around wildly, avoiding the low flying missiles.

Buckenbear rode his trained horse into the mass of orcs. Scattering them, he swung his weapon with great skill, each swing killing several orcs. The creatures, however much they outnumbered, were being held back; the Source was managing to help. Alanthos had re-mounted and was taking his horse back into the crowds. Just upon reaching the mass of creatures the horse had gone into a panic, and only his skill of horsemanship held him in the saddle. Several wild-cat-like creatures had torn through the scattering mass of orcs. The Sleepers twisted here and there, snapping at creatures and using their whips to send men falling from their horses as they fought to control them. In the panic several had died, and eventually Alanthos was thrown from his horse, hitting the floor hard and having the wind knocked out of him. The Sleepers had not stopped to kill him but had sped on towards the gates. One Sleeper had died on the approach as several arrows tore into it from the various archers darted about the battlefield. The others ripped into the walls and the already weakened gates in a desperate fashion. Only the highly trained minds of Theorn and Xendon managed to keep the troops defending with some success. Xendon sent several small packages down into their midst, annoying them and injuring them. The Sleepers climbed the walls only to be knocked down again. Slowly the troops killed them one by one. One had climbed and entered before being killed by three men. Still the city held the enemy at bay!

Slassiantha sat the enthusiastic guards down and began telling them of the dangers of creating creatures. She told them that to create a creature it must be real in their mind; there was no compromise in that. If not created properly the creature could turn on the caster, or the spell could disperse into the caster and temporarily disable or even kill. All was silent as she spoke. All the Zinobians knew of her knowledge and had begun to trust her judgement. A few of the other Zinobians had crept closer to eavesdrop and seemed interested. Morning Dew smiled a knowing smile and watched intently. Slassiantha gave a reassuring smile then concentrated, allowing the flows of power to wash over her: before her eyes a small rodent appeared and glowed in a golden haze. The rodent stood there, then sniffed the air and turned, and ran off into the distance before Slassiantha allowed the spell to diminish.

"Let me watch you create a small rodent first." Slassiantha spoke in a quiet warning tone. "Picture the rodent, picture it in every detail."

Slowly and somewhat reluctantly the guards rose to their feet, the first reluctance ever seen in a Zinobian as far as Slassiantha had seen. One Zinobian, a tall dark haired woman of middle age, concentrated, hard beads of sweat appearing on her forehead. Other joined in, all concentrating and watching with mixed emotions. Soon some wavering forms appeared before their eyes, various rodents of size and colour glowed and flickered. Some stayed for a short while before disappearing, some left as they appeared. One turned and attacked a younger guard; it threw its tiny body at the guard, knocking her down. Magic held more power than normal and the size made no difference. Slassiantha reacted quickly and before the teeth could penetrate, causing major harm, the creature disappeared in a puff of smoke. The guard lay on the floor in shock and surprise. Slowly she rose to her feet in an angry fashion, giving warning eyes to her fellow guards. The other guards diverted their eyes and continued to concentrate.

The Catchers stood a short distance away, watching the party with a sense of caution about them. Their burgundy bodies could easily be seen between their black spikes that hang neatly to the contours of their bodies and bobbed with their breathing. With keen yellow eyes they watched every movement made by the party. Catchers gave off a regal yet friendly appearance, highly magical as well. The elderly Catcher had a strong interest in Kerstan and his eyes had not left Kerstan in an unblinking fashion. Kerstan was conscious of the Catcher's stare and felt some of its feelings too. Shuddering unconsciously, he looked gently from Catcher to Catcher before he spoke.

"Firstly, we honour you and thank you for honouring us with your presence." Bowing slightly he continued. "Please allow me to explain of our reasons for this intrusion."

The Catchers sat lightly and seemed to relax a little as Kerstan spoke.

"The Source spoke to me as She touched me, She told me that you still lived and said She needs to speak with you urgently."

The Catchers looked among themselves then back at Kerstan.

"She has also asked if She can speak to you through me firstly."

Kerstan at this point stopped and took a deep breath before continuing, and studied the Catchers as he did. The Catchers still sat quietly but a mixture of expressions covering their faces.

"First She says sorry to Zandibar."

The older Catcher stepped back, shaken by the name, before correcting himself.

"Secondly She needs you to restore Her to full health to protect Catchers and man once again."

Kerstan shook violently and seemed to be in a trance, memory after memory flooded his brain. Him and Slassiantha mixing remedies, him laughing at a joke, a battle against trolls, so on and so on. Mutley and the Zinobians watched him closely, yet he still stood waiting for an answer. The older Catcher was pacing up and down, his spikes erect and angry, his features full of anguish.

"Man is no good, I tell you."

His voice shook with emotion as he spoke, Kerstan was going deeper into the trance and his body became angelic; his features were shining brightly like the Source itself.

"Please forgive me. I thought better of man."

The voice came from Kerstan, yet was not his voice, his mouth had not moved! All people around heard the voice load and clearly. The older Catcher (Zandibar) looked more troubled than before. His old body twisted in an agonising fashion and his face screwed up in anguish. His spikes stood so erect Mutley looked on worried they may lose themselves and hit someone.

"They killed her after all we did, they killed her!"

Zandibar's face was wet from tears and his colour had deepened considerably, he looked worn and old once again.

"Please I NEED your help, I am dying!"

As the words left Kerstan's mouth, hanging heavy in the air, he collapsed to the floor semi-conscious. The Catchers moved instantly before even the Zinobians reacted. Gathering around his body, they moved close to protect him. Zandibar tenderly touched his skin, power left his body and smothered Kerstan, and a gentle yellow glow lingered for several seconds before it dissipated back to normal. Kerstan's colour returned to his face slowly and he began to stir. Mutley pushed through the gathering and gently aided Kerstan to his feet. Slowly his focus returned and he looked weary yet alright. Zandibar took one step forward and spoke in a quiet voice.

"Yes we will go and see Her again, and I forgive Her."

Zandibar took on a younger look again; as he spoke a queer smile was on his face.

Maxinton approached the High Chief's chamber in a slow, deliberate fashion. Knowing the task before him would not be easy, he had gone over his speech several times. Once again he went over it in his mind as he neared. Upon reaching a set of heavy oak doors with ornate bronze patterns to the edge, he checked his armour was straight and in a clean state. Knocking loudly on the door he waited for a reply; he did not have to wait long. Presently a guard opened the door, his huge frame blocking a view into the chamber. The guard was at least twice the size of Maxinton and held an angry look. Looking him over quickly, the guard answered in a glib fashion.

"What brings you here, Maxinton?"

His voice did not disguise his annoyance at the disturbance.

"I would like to speak to the Chief to report."

Maxinton spoke with authority, giving the impression that he was expected. The guard's eyebrow raised a little as he thought about the request, and shutting the door tight again he left to speak to the Chief. Maxinton waited in the semi-dark trying to look official; several minutes passed then the guard returned. The door opened abruptly, making Maxinton jump slightly. The guard smiled at Maxinton, his face straightened again, and the guard spoke.

"Your audience has been granted, but make it brief."

Maxinton nervously straightened his armour again then entered the doors. Once inside the doors a thin dimly lit corridor led to another chamber with another door in it, and yet another guard as annoyed as the first sat in front of the door. As Maxinton entered the chamber the guard rose to his feet sword at the ready. The guard quickly took Maxinton's weapon then allowed him to enter. Maxinton entered slowly and took a look around the room. The room was a large room clad with finery. Leather of bright colours and furs hung from the far wall. On another was a huge menacing mace crossed with a just as menacing spear. The other had a blazing fire on it. A small spit had a rabbit turning over the fire. A young giant sat turning the spit absent-mindedly. To the centre of the chamber was a huge table made of stone and a large comfy chair. The chair had several large furs tossed over it and seated on the furs was the Chief. He was a man of at least eleven feet tall and his arms and legs resembled Shadma's: as thick as tree trunks. His body was covered in the tell-tale signs of battle and hard graft. Upon Maxinton entering, the Chief had leant forward slightly and placed his head gently on one of his huge hands. In a bored way, he gestured that Maxinton should speak. Maxinton stood straight and adjusted his armour again, then spoke in an authoritative way.

"Sire, I have interrogated heavily and feel after doing so that the news Shadma has brought is both valid and real."

Maxinton took a deep breath and continued; the young giant slowed in turning the spit then ladled some oil onto the rabbit before continuing. "As Shadma is my cousin I would like to help."

Maxinton, upon finishing, had made a low bow and was holding it, waiting for an answer. The answer came quick and harshly.

"You feel we should help little folk! Wasn't it them that disgraced us in the first place?"

Maxinton answered in a rather more angry tone than he had meant. "He is my cousin and I trust his judgment."

The Chief's face gave Maxinton a hard stare then a small smile crossed his face.

"Cousin or not, he lives with little folk so no, we do not help!"

Maxinton rose to confront but was stopped by the Chief speaking again.

"Go now and pester me no more."

The guard had appeared and taking Maxinton by the arm guided him out of the chamber. Maxinton stood outside and sighed; shaking his head he made his way back to talk to Shadma and Tinden.


The huge battle horse bucked and kicked under the command of Buckenbear; several goblins fell as the hooves hit them. Alanthos had left the main battle, turning his horse to head for the battlements. Sleepers were desperately attacking the battlements, trying to traverse the walls. One Sleeper had accomplished it and fought its way towards the magic it felt in the chapel. The city folk had fought their fear and were desperately fighting the Sleeper, slowing its movement. Theorn, seeing his chance, had thrown himself off the watchtower onto the Sleeper; upon landing his short elfin assassin knife had embedded itself deep into the shoulder of the Sleeper. The blade snapped upon impact and sat deep in the shoulder. Grabbing the Sleeper's head, he had twisted using his weight and toppled the Sleeper. The Sleeper fell twisted then stood again; several spears dug deep into the Sleeper where it fell, its underside was more vulnerable and had taken several hits. One Sleeper died. Two more were left and still attacked the city.

To no avail the archers defended the walls, with amazing stealth the Sleepers climbed the wall. Over the top they came, sweeping city folk off the towers as they went. With whips in claws they attacked, killing and maiming many men, using their fear attack to scatter and confuse all in their path. Horses tethered reared and snorted in fear, children ran and screamed, and even the men were panic filled. The Sleepers pushed on towards the magic they now could sense vividly. City folk fought bravely, using anything at hand to slow the creatures. Xendon sent fire from his staff and slowed their path. Theorn, back on his feet, began helping in the attack. Into his robe Xendon plunged his arm, pulling out the leaf with the last of the black ooze in; holding it tightly he made his way closer to the maddened Sleeper. Its body thrashed this way and that, whip catching man after man, teeth snapping. Slowly he neared his opponent, then threw the leaf at the broadside of the Sleeper. Black sticky ooze clung to its side.

"Step away NOW!"

As Xendon yelled he rushed at the Sleeper. The Sleeper turned to face the advancing man, its teeth bared. City folk ran in all directions to enlarge the gap. Flames shot from Xendon's staff as he dived past the Sleeper. The flame, upon hitting the ooze, caused an explosion that threw the Sleeper in a rough arc across the floor. Green ooze and flesh went all over the place; the Sleeper fell and span then slowly rose to its feet again. With great effort the Sleeper moved with less speed at Xendon. Whip in claw, it sent the end at Xendon, whipping his feet from under him. Moving at a pace the Sleeper pounced over Xendon, on towards the chapel. The other Sleeper was under heavy attack from all directions, the men stabbing at its armour. Although the Sleeper killed several men it died quickly. Bleeding badly, the remaining Sleeper made its way towards the chapel. Nothing that the men did seemed to stop it, closer and closer it got. From the entrance of the chapel as the Sleeper neared came a Zenithe. The Zenithe seemed to float across towards the Sleeper, its white robe flowing gently in the breeze. Soon the robe hung heavy in the rain and the Zenithe and Sleeper stood within a few feet from each other. The Zenithe blocked the way for the Sleeper and had an annoyed look about it.

The Sleeper circled then pounced; the Zenithe knocked it aside with ease. Again the Sleeper pounced, this time taking hold of the arm of the Zenithe. The Zenithe and Sleeper soon rolled and threw each other about. Every movement was a glide and seemed as if no effort was made; city folk stood their ground waiting for an opening. The Zenithe managed to throw the Sleeper clear again but had a large gash across its white robe; blood freely flowed, covering the front. The Sleeper crouched and slowly circled the Zenithe once again, this time with confidence, ever watchful of other attack. The Zenithe began circling too and raised its arms to create a light glow that hung in the air. The Sleeper and the Zenithe weighed each other carefully up and down. The Sleeper pounced and as it did the glow left the Zenithe, engulfing the Sleeper. The Sleeper shook on the floor then began to rise again. City folk used the opportunity and joined in the fight, killing the Sleeper. Once it was dead the Zenithe staggered around as if all its energy was gone; stumbling, the Zenithe righted its body smoothly, stumbled again, and then fell to die in a pool of its own blood. The battle was fierce and the city was being taken over. How much longer could the men defend against the vast armies? The battlements were covered in creatures bent on destroying the city. However, the Source still defended to some avail.

Morning Dew stood tall and full of determination, her eyes fixed ahead, her mouth held in a tight fashion. Slassiantha watched, sat nearby on a small rock. They had left the camp and travelled a short distance to be free from prying eyes. The teaching was going well and Morning Dew had created a chicken and a goat successfully, now she attempted a wild boar. Slassiantha had said it was time to try something that could turn nasty if not controlled. Morning Dew had been ready to try and started straight away. Her face tightened up into a grimace and she squealed with delight as the boar began to appear. Flickering in and out of visibility, the boar watched her closely. Soon it appeared stronger and then turned and left in the opposite direction after a chicken; both disappeared under a chuckle from Slassiantha as she watched. Slassiantha looked on and felt proud of the way Morning Dew had developed her skills.

"You are doing great."

As she spoke Morning Dew glanced across and the boar flickered and vanished. Cross at herself, Morning Dew attempted to try again. Suddenly the sound of approaching feet stopped them both. From around the dirt mound came Greatbird who smiled upon seeing them both.

"I thought I heard you laughing." Greatbird smiled strongly and lovingly at Morning Dew, then at Slassiantha.

"Greatbird, nice evening isn't it?"

Slassiantha's voice was straining to sound natural and she smiled innocently at Greatbird. Greatbird smiled back in a relaxed manner and looking around casually, walked slowly over to where they now stood.

"What is going on here, you two spend a lot of time together?"

Greatbird's tone was one of teasing and relaxed Slassiantha enough to answer.

"She was asking for an update on the training."

Greatbird gave a satisfied smile and returned to her lazy gazing over the mountainous scenery. Several seconds passed before she spoke again, as she did her eyes still looked absently out over the surrounding area.

"Your friends have been gone a while."

Slassiantha found her thoughts went to Kerstan and Mutley. She joined Greatbird in absently staring at the mountains.


Kerstan, Mutley and the Zinobians walked slowly in the direction the Catchers had taken. Mixed thoughts crossed their minds as they walked. Can we trust them, what happens now, where are we going?

After a short while they came upon an opening between some rocks. Once beyond the rocks the land opened up into a wide open-plan field. The whole field was full of yellow rapeseed and shone brightly in the sunshine. Blinking to clear the vision, the party continued to follow. Slowly the Catchers led the group into the field. As the centre became closer a small camp could be made out, made up of mud and twigs delicately crafted into mounds that housed a small colony of Catchers. A slight glow of a golden colour hung around the area. The closer the party got to the camp the more they felt the magic. Their hairs on their necks began to stand on end and their skin prickled. The Zinobian women had slowed and were showing strong signs of caution. Drawing their weapons they continued behind Mutley and Kerstan. They both still moved closer and as yet had not drawn their weapons.

Once in the camp Kerstan looked upon what could be the last of the Catchers, nine in number. Kerstan was grateful to see that one or two showed signs of pregnancy. Upon entering the camp the Catchers had gathered close together and held their spikes erect and guardedly. Zandibar spoke to the other Catchers in a quiet strange tongue and soon they visibly calmed. It was not long before all were welcome in the camp and calm was restored. Plans were made that after a meal later in the evening they would all leave, other than the pregnant Catchers and one other. They would take as quick a route as they could to get to the Source. However, they would stop off and collect Slassiantha on route. Soon a small fire was lit and a strange soup made of various roots bubbled on the fire. It smelt fabulous and Mutley rubbed his hands in anticipation. Sitting around the fire Kerstan spoke to Zandibar and the other Catchers. Soon the younger Catchers were asking for stories of old to be told and Mutley and Kerstan obliged with telling stories that were full of action and battles. This continued as the food was served and on through the meal.

The gates of Greatoak shook on their hinges once again. Huge rams were being used to barge their way into the city. Orcs and trolls pushed and shoved at the great gate to no avail. Arrows were shot into the fray and several fell only to be replaced by another attack. Alanthos and the other horsemen were trying to create a break in the attack, but getting through the mass of creatures seamed near impossible. Xendon had joined Buckenbear on horseback and was fighting furiously to weaken the attack. The rain was still hammering down, blinding the creatures and men below. Large lightning flashes shook the ground upon impact and filled the red sky with light. The clouds were black and heavy and loomed low over the battle. The ground was thick with mud and sticky to move in. Still the creatures outnumbered the citizens by ten to one. The city defences still miraculously held under the Source's protection but for how long? Inside the chapel the Source was in disarray, bits had crumbled as decay set in. Several large areas lay in open wounds that the Zenithe fought to repair. Zenithes lay exhausted or dead from the exertion of keeping the Source alive. The only hope was for the Catchers to arrive and repair it with their knowledge and magical skill. Even if they arrived, how would they pass the mass of battle to get to the Source?

Shadma moved awkwardly from one elbow to the other, wincing slightly as he did so. He and Tinden sat amongst the other giants eating what was to be their last meal before leaving to return to the city to help in any way they could. They had decided that they had to leave, even if it was alone; time was too short to wait and try to persuade the giants to help. However, both sat eating the meal of roasted oxen in a relaxed manner. Shadma had suggested that it was best to leave without showing their disappointment at the others' attitudes. Maxinton had chosen to sit with them and show his approval. All sat eating in a happy mood. Conversation was about Shadma and his life away from camp with the humans. This conversation was gracefully being listened to without too many adverse comments. Shadma was halfway through a sentence when Tinden rose to his feet quickly and sniffed the air. He began staring in rapid movements in all directions, sniffing wildly. Several giants had stopped listening and watched with a curious fashion. It was Shadma who spoke.

"What? What's wrong, Tinden?"

Shadma rose slowly in a worried and tense fashion as he spoke, eyes fixed on Tinden. Tinden seemed to ignore Shadma and was frantically sniffing the air. Looking everywhere in a quick fashion he suddenly shouted at the top of his voice.

"Trolls! They are heading this way, several of them!"

All the giants stared at Tinden, slowly all rose to their feet in a disbelieving fashion. All looked in the direction Tinden was staring, a few seconds passed and then the trolls appeared.

Their heavily armoured rubbery-skinned bodies seemed to keep coming more and more, all heavily armed with swords or maces. The trolls smashed their way through the camp. Several large fires were started and huts burned, taking with them livestock and food. Soon the camp was awash with trolls; a small army had come across the camp on route to the city. Several giants died, taken by surprise, and several others were injured before the giants returned with their own attack. Each mighty blow made by a giant would send two or three trolls scattering like skittles. The battle was fierce and quick, the death toll high. Once the battle ended and the last of the trolls lay dead, the surviving giants surveyed the camp. The village lay in virtual destruction. Smouldering huts had part of their roofs missing; fences were destroyed and livestock was everywhere. Dead lay in all directions.

Shadma was breathing heavily from his part in the battle and had a nasty gash across his right thigh. Tinden was nowhere to be seen.

Soon, from a tall tree nearby, Tinden lowered himself. Once he had seen the trolls he had used his nimble arms and legs to climb the tree and there he had stayed, holding on for his life.

"We fight! Yes we go with you and we fight!"

The voice had come from one giant nearby and was echoed swiftly by others. The voice had been from the Chief, and he stood up strongly and shook with rage. Upon finishing his voice rose to an almighty yell.

"Arachnor marithton!"

Soon the air was full of the battle cry as all the giants as one, Shadma included, yelled. The earth shook under the noise.


As the day drew into evening the Zinobians began finishing their many tasks. They would then make their way back to enjoy the meal that was being prepared at the moment by the men back at camp. Slassiantha took the opportunity and motioned to Morning Dew to follow away to practise some more. Morning Dew's progress was good: the bear that she was creating was vivid and responded well to her leading. Slassiantha reacted quickly before Morning Dew stopped the creation. A huge serpent appeared and its huge muscular body tried to wind itself around the bear; both fought to beat the other. The serpent coiled itself tight around the bear's waist; Morning Dew gasped for air then concentrated hard and the bear pulled the serpent free. Sweat ran freely down both of their faces as the battle continued. The serpent slowly gained the winning move, pinning the bear to the ground. The bear wriggled and fought before disappearing. Morning Dew collapsed to the floor and, although exhausted by the battle, began laughing uncontrollably. Slassiantha settled down next to her and began laughing also. Both lay there exhausted before Slassiantha spoke.

"That was great! You are doing great."

As Slassiantha spoke she slapped Morning Dew heartedly on the back. Morning Dew looked at Slassiantha and the smile left her face, an angry look taking its place. Slassiantha backed away speaking quickly.

"Sorry, I didn't mean to offend you, but that was great."

Slowly the smile returned to her face and then both laughed again.

"Enough tonight, I think. You look exhausted."

Rising to her feet, Slassiantha held her hand out to help Morning Dew to her own. Morning Dew gave a look and rose on her own, speaking harshly.

"I am alright, thanks."

Smiling again she turned and made her way back to the camp. Slassiantha smiled after her and made to follow slowly, deep in thought.

"Do you feel its time to tell Greatbird?"

The words had left her mouth before she realised she had spoken. Cringing slightly she waited for the answer. Morning Dew stopped and turned slowly to look at Slassiantha. Slassiantha waited at a distance for the answer.

"Yes, I do feel it may be time."

Morning Dew spoke with authority but absent-mindedly. She looked like an adult and nothing like the small girl she was. Slassiantha joined her and both moved towards the camp once again. Entering the camp, they watched the Zinobians and took in the smells of the meal. Slassiantha smiled at Morning Dew and turned towards the Chief's hut, followed by Morning Dew. She had taken only two steps when she stopped abruptly upon hearing her name. Turning towards the voice Slassiantha saw entering at the far side of the camp Kerstan, Mutley and the Zinobians. Then a short while later a few burgundy creatures entered also. Their tiny bodies glided in a delicate fashion. Slassiantha began running towards the party. The Catchers scattered in all directions, spikes erect and ready, their movements quick and effortless.

Kerstan took Slassiantha in his strong arms and hugged her hard. Standing there, they both held each other as tears rolled down Slassiantha's face. Through the tears she spoke.

"I feared that I would never see you again."

Kerstan just held her sobbing body tightly to him and smiled.


Alanthos swung a wide arc with his sword, slicing a gap in the creatures to move in. Several fell to the ground, others taking their place. Sweat poured down his face but sheer determination prevented him slowing. Buckenbear stood beside him, his battleaxe causing great casualties with each blow. Xendon had moved his mount into the middle and was fighting with magic and sword. All around the battle raged, and the weather continued to complement the anger shown from both sides. The rain was hammering down and refused to ease, the clouds loomed low and black in the red sky, and the lightning still fell, killing and maiming. The evening light was diminishing and the lightning helped in lighting the battle. All along the battlements, torches were lit and glowed wearily in the darkness, constantly threatened by the rain. Showers of arrows rained onto the battle scene each time lightning lit their passage. The Source had felt an evil presence approaching and had called on more power; shining wildly the Source sent protection out and healed the injured. The Zenithe struggled with the increase.

Snode pushed his war horse as he neared the hill. The battle was easily heard now and scouts had reported that the edge was just over the hill. Snode moved to resettle himself on the saddle, his tail wrapping itself around the hind leg of the horse. The staff shone its eerie glow and red flashes hit the clouds. Instantly the rain thickened and more lightning fell. An evil cackle left his mouth and he spurred on the horse once again. From the battlements the archers fired accurate arrows, killing and slowing the attack. Theorn looked out and saw in the distance Snode sitting on his horse. His evil was almost tangible and Theorn shuddered, shouting commands he regained his composure. Desperation in his movements, he continued to send arrow after arrow into the fray. Suddenly a huge blood-curdling cry was heard from the east. With keen eyes Theorn looked in horror towards the sound, and as he eyes focused his expression changed. Over the hill came a huge army of giants led by Shadma and Tinden. Watching, he saw their huge frames tearing into the rear of the battle. Orcs and goblins flew in every direction with every blow. Slowly the surprise was lost and the creatures began to fight back. Soon the giants were outnumbered and struggled even with their height advantage. Snode shot huge balls of fire into the array of creatures from his staff, killing many with each strike. His army began pushing closer to the city once again.

Slassiantha sat close to Kerstan as they ate the meal that was presented before them. Greatbird had been happy to see their return and was sitting nearby, eating thoughtfully and listening to the tale of their journey. All was quiet in the camp again, all training had stopped and the women sat being served by the men. Once the meal was served the men sat at a distance to wait to serve again then eat after what was left. It was at the request of Slassiantha that Kerstan and Mutley ate with them. Morning Dew sat and watched the Catchers wide eyed. She had a plate full of food in front of her that had not been touched. The Catchers were eating heartily and seemed relaxed in the camp. Everyone ate the meal quickly and conversation was plentiful. Once finished, the women stood and left to return to their tasks. The men gathered the food left and ate their fill also. Kerstan and Slassiantha strode off together with Greatbird and Morning Dew. Greatbird took Slassiantha aside and spoke quietly to her in private.

"You sleep here tonight, leave tomorrow."

As she spoke she indicated that the invitation was to Kerstan and Mutley also. Slassiantha smiled reassuringly then spoke.

"No, we must leave quickly. The city needs our help."

Greatbird looked from Slassiantha to Kerstan, her face giving little of her thoughts away. Slassiantha studied her while considering her next move. After a few seconds of silence she spoke again.

"Greatbird."

Greatbird seemed to notice Slassiantha for the first time, coming out of her dream-like state.

"Please come and fight along with us, we will need your courage and great skill to win this battle, I fear."

Greatbird gazed at Slassiantha with unusual compassion, weighing up the answer she would give. After a long gaze at Kerstan and the Catchers she answered with a sense of regret about her.

"Our place is here, not with you."

Her voice was heavy and sad, yet full of authority.

"I will go and fight!"

Slassiantha spun to the voice; Morning Dew had rose from her place at the fireside and was approaching her as she spoke.

"You are too young and must stay here."

Morning Dew moved angrily at Slassiantha and spat the words straight in her face. "I am ready and I want to go."

Her voice was full of anger, yet her body was under total control. Greatbird looked at them both and moved to separate the quarrel. Stopping in her tracks, Greatbird stood in mixed emotions; before her eyes a huge fiery Roc had appeared, its huge frame was one of fire and glowed brightly. Its eyes were focused on both Slassiantha and herself. Slassiantha gave no indication of worry as she rounded on the Roc. Instantly the bird wavered, flickered, yet remained standing still before them both. Morning Dew smiled at both of them then shutting her eyes allowed the Roc to dissipate and then vanish. Greatbird stood and looked on in astonishment, even after the bird had gone she stood rigid to the floor, her body fixed ready to fight, her face full of pride and purpose, her muscles taut and ready to strike if necessary. Several Zinobians had risen and stood ready also. Morning Dew spoke in a triumphant way.

"I AM ready and I WILL be going."

As she spoke she eyed both menacingly.

Greatbird, ignoring her, turned towards Slassiantha who went to try to explain. Across Greatbird's face was a broad smile.

"You have taught her well, for that I am grateful."

Slassiantha gave a low and respectful bow in reply; Kerstan had approached and placing his strong arm on Slassiantha's shoulder he spoke apologetically.

"Slassiantha, we must leave soon if Zandibar is going to be able to help the Source, if we are not too late."

Greatbird stepped forward and, taking the arm of Slassiantha in a tight and powerful grip, spoke.

"Yes you go! And for teaching Morning Dew, we go too."

Turning and raising her arms in a triumphant way she continued in a loud voice.

"We go and we win, beating the enemies of Slassiantha."

The camp became one of triumphant yells of war and courage as the Zinobians rose in response to the cry.


The rain was coming thick and fast, clouds as black as the night that was drawing in but with the usual red tinge to them. Lightning shot its evil attacks on the mass below, scattering and killing with each blow it made. As far as the eye could see creatures fought against humans in an attempt to destroy their heritage. Mingled amongst the many were men of a huge size, giants in every sense of the word. The battle was endless and only seemed to slow to then build up into a more fierce attack in the next moment. The ground was now a boggy mass of carnage and sucked the strength from the many that walked its paths. Dead and injured lay arrayed in all directions, uncared for in the battle's intensity.


Snode had ridden deep into the fray and, upon his war horse, now used his evil magic at its highest level. The twisted staff with the thorns glowed almost constantly as bolt after bolt left destruction in its path; men dropped like the rain about them. The arrival of Snode had produced intensity to the attack as the creatures took comfort in his formidable presence. The Source was aware of him too and had poured its protection heavily upon the city men to try to beat the attack; its power however was failing and decay was beginning to have its way with the mass of honeycomb, causing large splits to form. The Zenithe fought bravely to correct this and so far had accomplished their task to a reasonable level. However the task had its price: several lay dead, others exhausted by their efforts. The bough of the mighty oak had taken the strain and had begun to suffer also. Its bark was drying and cracks began to appear along its rough surface.

Snode turned his horse and sent yet another bolt into the fray; several men scattered under the blast, lying in the destruction to breath their last. Xendon, high upon his horse, turned his horse into the fray, chopping a path through to head for Snode. Anger on his normally calm face, he pushed the horse onward through the resistance that occurred; with blow after blow creatures in his path were being knocked aside. The gap slowly shortened. Snode, unaware of his approach, continued to fire his evil. Buckenbear was fighting hard too and causing the mass of creatures around him to scatter or die under his mighty weapon.

Xendon felt the evil as he neared Snode's formidable presence; now in close proximity to him he raised his staff. Knocking two creatures aside he sent a bolt of yellow light directly at his unaware enemy. Xendon had put every ounce of experience and power into the attack, and as the bolt left his staff it seemed to scream out and shone like the lightning around it. The bolt's power was felt by all it passed; several fell, knocked physically to the ground as it passed. Others momentarily slowed in attack to glance towards Xendon in awe of the magic. The bolt, upon hitting Snode hard in the shoulder blades, threw Snode clear off his now startled horse. The horse spun and kicked out in panic, injuring several creatures. Hitting the floor hard, Snode lay awkwardly, winded and in considerable pain; his staff had been thrown several feet away from him.

Xendon felt queasy and wanted to be sick as he forced himself to stay upright on his horse. Sending another bolt at Snode, he fought on. Snode used his great strength to push himself slowly to his feet, thrown sideways with each bolt sent. The bolts were loosing power and eventually he stood and made his way to the staff. The creatures, unsure of the action to take, had made an arc around the mighty battle, not to be hit by the power being displayed. As Snode's leathery hand was about to grip its staff, Xendon fired another bolt. The bolt hit square in the jaw and sent Snode sprawling to the floor in pain. Xendon was now in full concentration, both in staying conscious under the strain and in the destruction of evil itself. Although feeling sick and dizzy, Xendon had the advantage and was determined to use it. Snode sent a wave of power at Xendon; without his staff it was weakened however it pushed Xendon, making his horse rear and stumble. As the horse righted itself Xendon fought to stay in the saddle. Concentration left Snode long enough for the staff to be gained once again. Facing Snode, Xendon had just enough time to see the bolt before being knocked from the horse.

Xendon, with great skill, landed squarely on his feet and, using his momentum, rolled to safety from the next bolt sent. Both tired, they squared up against each other. Snode leaned heavily on his staff, glaring angrily across at Xendon. Xendon was bleeding badly from a gash across his forehead and lay heavily, also on his staff. Snode began to mutter words, his mouth moving quickly. Xendon, unable to hear, waited for the outcome. Nothing came so Xendon forced his body forward and drew his sword from its sheath. Snode gave an evil smile and waited. Each step seamed to take ages but the gap shortened quickly. Xendon, upon nearing, raised his sword, putting all the skill he had into the blow.

From the corner of his eye he saw the movement. Too late to defend against the attack, Xendon fell. Several city men fell as the wild-cat-like body twisted and leapt clear of their bodies, its victim unaware of its approach. Called by its master, the Sleeper had turned and come. Its grotesque body covered in sores knocked Xendon to the floor, its teeth tight around his unguarded neck. Hitting the floor, the Sleeper turned and attacked again. The attack was unnecessary as the head was free from the body. Xendon lay dead where the creature had hit him. City folk, angered by their loss, quickly destroyed the Sleeper. Snode, although tired, turned and continued to fight.

Alanthos and Buckenbear stood back-to-back using each other as a shield. Using every bit of skill gathered from their fighting wars of old, they cut into the mass of creatures. Orcs, goblins and trolls fell under the sting of their weapons. Alanthos was tiring, being the older of the two, yet with great skill Buckenbear defended and attacked for both of them, allowing him to rest a little.

Within the chapel the Zenithe worked in a hive of activity. Fearful now of the outcome for the Source, they continued to strive in their repairs.

So far the city walls had resisted the enemy, with only a few getting in now and then, but for how much longer? So far the Source had protected and empowered the men, so far the enemy had been held at bay.


Maxinton moved with a graceful motion, using his fine weapons with all the skill he had. Each swing found its mark and was effective in its task. Laughing, he swung more and revelled in such a decent battle and challenge. It had been a long time since he had last felt this challenged and it felt good. This was what he had trained to accomplish and he lived for the excitement.

Shadma moved with a smooth action for his size and bulk, his huge arms and legs swinging and diving this way and that, knocking creatures all over the place. He hit with such a force that they flew several feet with each blow. Everywhere the battle raged; the rain matching the battle's action. The rain fell in sheet form, obscuring the vision and stinging the skin; clouds as red as they had been no sign of slowing. With a great effort the trolls beat at the gates and finally the gates gave way. Orcs, goblins and trolls poured through the opening, attacking all who stood to stop them. The men fought hard and fast with little effect, losing numbers heavily. Theorn fired arrows in quick succession into the creatures, taking several creatures down to little effect. The city was now under attack and soon homes and stalls were being rampaged.

Morning Dew, holding the reins hard, leant over the broad wing of her Roc. Taking the hand of Slassiantha, she pulled hard and soon had her safely seated behind her. Slassiantha gripped hard with her feet and nervously felt the powerful muscles of the Roc beneath her body. Its feathers were course and had a waxy feel to them. The Roc looked over its shoulder with its keen eyes at Slassiantha and Morning Dew gently caressed the neck to calm the animal. With a gentle kick from her heel, the Roc stirred to life, rising swiftly and gracefully into the air. Kerstan and Mutley rode behind two other Zinobians; both looked at the other nervously as the Rocs took flight. The Rocs were magnificent birds and had the power to easily cope with the extra weight. Soon all were flying at an incredible pace, pushed on by their guides on their backs. The Zinobians seemed to be as one on the Rocs' backs and controlled them with ease. The flight was magnificent, the wind fresh in their faces. Kerstan admired the speed and grace of the birds, the height, and the view.

Slassiantha held on tightly and stared out across the land as it sped by. With the slightest movement a Zinobian could redirect their Roc, avoiding collisions accurately. Each Zinobian wore heavy leather armour and carried their preferred weapon just as finely made. Determination was in every move they made and the Rocs were moving at an incredible pace. Greatbird flew at the front with two massive guards flanking her every movement. Morning Dew was easily able to keep her Roc up with the main group, although it was younger. Smiling, she glanced over her shoulder at Slassiantha who was holding onto the feathers of the Roc so tightly that her fingers were white. Flying closeby on other Rocs were the Catchers, which seemed very relaxed and at one with the movement.

The land below was a mass of burnt-out villages and death and destruction; in the distance dark clouds were gathering. The air felt cool and threatened rain. There was a bad storm ahead and they were heading into it at quite a pace. The Zinobian warriors made no attempt to slow their rides and just continued to push on in determination. Every Zinobian held a look that said live or die: they would fight and fight hard. Soon the Rocs flew into the rain and the rain was coming down heavily. Still they flew on. Suddenly, from above a dark shadow flew in at incredible speed. A Zinobian, only by her quick reactions, managed to steer her Roc clear as a Drarghen flew past, narrowly missing the wing.

"Drarghen."

The Zinobian who spoke seemed to Slassiantha to be fearful. This was the first sign of weakness shown by a Zinobian. Soon the Rocs were flying in awkward angles with their passengers holding on for their lives. Three Drarghens were flying in and out of the formation of Rocs, picking off any slow Roc or rider. As one flew in a guard swung her axe hard, missing the neck of the Drarghen. Off balance, she tried to correct herself but was hit by its tail and sent spinning off the back of her Roc. One quick turn of the Drarghen's neck and only half of her body hit the ground below. Soon utter chaos was ensuing and Rocs and Drarghens flew in tight angles in close combat.

Slassiantha motioned to Morning Dew to fly straight then she began to concentrate, allowing the power to flow in her. Taking one hand off the Roc, she wobbled, put her hand back on, then tried again. Concentrating hard, she created a fiery Drarghen that flew into the crowd of creatures. The reaction was only short lived but was enough to help the Zinobians. The nearest Drarghen took a deep slice from a sword and tumbled towards the ground. The fiery Drarghen wavered and disappeared as Slassiantha collapsed heavily onto Morning Dew, causing the Roc to lunge briefly before being righted. Two Drarghens were left moving in and out, snapping up their prey. With ease, the huge frames swerved this way and that. With four Rocs dead or injured, the Zinobians fought on.

Drarghens were quick and deadly and flew able to change direction in quick jerky movements. This was something that a Roc could do if not carrying a passenger, but as they did have and precious ones, it was another thing. Rocs and Zinobians flew in hard arc after another; the movement took full concentration to stay on the Rocs but had to be made to keep both themselves and the Rocs alive. The Rocs carrying the Catchers and other non-tribal persons were soon bunched together in a dangerously close formation.

A Drarghen turned and flying low past one Roc tore deep with its claw into the underside of its victim as it narrowly missed collision with another. The reaction was instantaneous and the Roc bucked, throwing its rider high into the air. Another Zinobian was down. Slassiantha righted herself and gave an anxious look at the huge frames that flew with such ease of destruction. Weakened by her last efforts, she felt unsure of trying again with the movement as it was from her ride. Morning Dew glanced back and called to hold tight then swept low, leaving the others and arcing hard to the right, flying low around the mountains below. Finding what she wanted, she turned her Roc and flew to join the other Rocs once again. From where they were, Slassiantha and Morning Dew could see the Drarghens moving menacingly back and forth, at this moment unaware of them. Winking, she pointed at the mountains then at the Drarghens. Slassiantha raised her eyebrows at her and smiled back in puzzlement.

Suddenly, from below and at considerable speed, small rocks of variable sizes flew up past their vantage point and into the fray. Several seconds passed as the rocks hit their marks, blow after blow, knocking into the scales of the Drarghens as they flew this way and that. The distraction was swift and short, the results were enough. Zinobian warriors, taking full control, swung their weapons, killing the last Drarghens as they recovered from the surprise.

With the Drarghens gone, the Zinobians realised that the rain was heavy. Down below now the ground was soaked and boggy, covered with thousands of moving creatures of all types fighting each other. As they had fought they had flown over the battle and were now in the battle itself. Projectiles flew up at them, causing them to have to manoeuvre fast to avoid being hit. Giants could be seen fighting with ferocious movements; they seemed to be making some headway against the orcs they fought. The city soon came into view and the Zinobians flew on fast. Greatbird signalled and the party split into two groups. One group took Kerstan, Slassiantha and the Catchers, the other flew lower and soon the Zinobians were dismounting and engaging in battle.

The first group flew deeper into the battle, closer to the city. As they flew the Zinobians used their bows and killed accurately as they flew past, still able to steer to avoid projectiles. One or two took hits and fell to their death, or landed and fought. As they flew the Zinobian spoke quickly to their passengers, telling of what they intended. The Zinobian speaking to Zandibar was still talking, unaware that he had leapt from the Roc. Zandibar had stood angry and erect upon seeing his enemy. Leaping, he had landed smoothly, coping with the speed at which he hit the floor, rolling then regaining his feet in one smooth movement. With Snode in view, he made his way through the many creatures, killing all who stood in his way or simply rolling or jumping past them. Determination and anger moved his small yet agile body. Age forgotten, with anger as a friend, he pushed closer to Snode. Snode, unaware of his approach, was sending angry bolts into the battle, scattering his enemies each time. Zandibar was virtually upon him when he noticed his approach. Zandibar stood erect and angry before Snode. Snode, losing his angry look for one of surprise, soon recovered himself quickly.

"My you have grown, Zandibar! Come to join your parents?" Spitting out the last, he taunted Zandibar. Spikes erect and ready, Zandibar circled his foe.

Several seconds had passed before the other Zinobians had realised his dismount. Quickly they circled, scanning the ground. It didn't take long to see Zandibar heading quickly towards Snode. The Zinobians and Catchers dismounted to help him, as well as Kerstan, Slassiantha, Morning Dew and Greatbird. With expertise the Zinobians brought their Rocs close to the ground among the creatures. Once in their midst, the Roc skilfully slashed with their claws, gaining area for the dismount, and pecked at any creature that refused to move. Once their mount had left, they then took off again to fly in and out of the fray as an extra attack for their mistress. This action took all of a few seconds and resulted in little if any damage being taken by all involved. Once on the ground and in one smooth movement, the Zinobian would slice the nearest creature and then swiftly move onto the next, the entire time heading in the direction of Zandibar. It took only a short time for two other Catchers to join Zandibar in circling Snode, who was now fully focused on Zandibar.

Zandibar controlled his anger and the urge to avenge his parents and continued to circle Snode in a menacing manner. One of the other Catchers, a young Catcher, was not so slow in attacking: swiftly the Catcher raised his spikes and lunged in a deep arc at the legs of Snode. His movement was fast and fierce yet not fast enough. Snode, upon seeing the movement, raised his staff and sent a venomous bolt of energy at the ground in front of the Catcher; dirt and mud splattered in all directions. The Catcher lost its footing, rolled to regain himself, and fell heavily into the hole before righting himself once again. A second bolt was sent and this time at the young Catcher himself. Unprepared and unable to defend, the blow hit his small frame, sending huge shocks of pain throughout his body. Rising slowly he flung himself forward in attack once again; both Zandibar and the other helped in distracting his focus off the youngster.

Snode seemed at ease with the attacks and sent several bolts preventing any advancement from them. Zandibar held back and circled once again as the other two continued to attack, both spikes raised and ready. The second Catcher, a larger and more experienced one, had managed to gain the ground needed to make his attack. With a mighty leap, he threw his body with incredible force at Snode. Upon impact, his spikes erect and angry, he hit Snode hard on the arm, knocking him off balance before releasing once again. Loose flesh and puss flew off freely. With a smooth movement he landed, rolled, and turned to attack again. Zandibar waited for his opportunity and continued to circle.

The younger one was back in the attack and jumped with its spikes raised; Snode sent a bolt at it as it flew at him. Zandibar took his chance and dived across the line of fire, spikes raised and ready to receive the bolt. Energy soared into his veins; power and magic touched his body and sent restoring vibrations searing through him. The younger Catcher smiled at Zandibar and gave a small wink before moving on again. Zandibar took on a different form: his body grew and became more muscular and agile. Looking younger once again, he circled Snode again. The first, upon regaining his footing, had moved back into attack once again. Using the younger's distraction to his advantage, he threw his body heavily once again at Snode.

Spikes lay deep in Snode's back as the Catcher flew past; this time the Catcher did not retract his spikes but tried to pull Snode off his feet. Snode screamed in anger and agony, swayed but righted himself, tearing the now vulnerable Catcher free then taking a deep bite into his underside, throwing the limp body aside. The younger attacked fast once again, slicing at his feet with his spikes. Snode was beginning to slow and showed signs that the attacks were working.

Another bolt shot from Snode's staff and once again Zandibar took the bolt intended for the youngster. Zandibar was now a huge creature of enormous size and stature. Magic soared through his veins, eagerly awaiting its release. The younger Catcher had to work fast now, keeping the attention of Snode. Rolling quickly, he flung his injured body high across the path of Snode, spikes erect and ready. At the same instant Zandibar took his chance and sent all the power gained from his body. White light lit the area; ground all around quaked and flew in all directions. Creatures hit the ground with force as the power shot past them. The younger Catcher, spikes high ready to receive, bathed in the edges of the power, its full force hitting Snode squarely in his main torso. With incredible force the whiter light threw his frame high into the air, shook it, then exploded into thousands of pieces. Flesh and puss dissolved the intense power, destroying all it hit. All that remained to mark Snode's presence was his staff lying in the dirt. Upon the impact from the attack, the staff had been let go of and had fallen harmlessly to the ground. Lying there, it had lost its eerie glow and lay still. Soon the mud and bog swallowed the staff out of sight.

Just then a Sleeper appeared, drawn by the power crazed by the magic. It attacked Zandibar, who was still vulnerable. Zandibar rolled and hit the floor hard. The Sleeper turned to attack again, but took a heavy blow from the younger Catcher in the chest. A huge slice followed this swiftly, from the battleaxe of a Zinobian warrior who had joined the battle. The Sleeper shook then died. Bruised and with a nasty cut, Zandibar rose to his feet once again.

Slassiantha, upon leaving her mount, sent blow after blow into the fray. Determination took her onward. She had to get to Zandibar and save him from injury. Kerstan was close behind, slicing hard left and right. Morning Dew, once Slassiantha was clear of the Roc, pounced from her place on the Roc's back. As she came to land, her sword flashed in a wide arc; two orcs lay dead, a third followed as she hit the floor, the sword spinning out of the arc into a deep chop, slicing it in two down to its belt. Rolling, she braced herself ready to attack again if necessary. Off at a pace she went in pursuit of Kerstan and Slassiantha. Greatbird was not far behind, leaving her mount in a flip, taking three orcs with her axe and then burying it deep in the shoulders of a troll. Quickly retrieving her weapon she followed Morning Dew, keeping her in view the whole time. Creatures were everywhere and the passage proved a slow one.

Slassiantha could see the fight occur move by move and desperately made her way closer. Progress was going well until a troll stood in her path; Kerstan rushed past, chopping at the troll which staggered before advancing injured towards Slassiantha. Morning Dew suddenly appeared in mid-air, her sword held high, a war cry loud on her lips. The troll fell awkwardly to the floor, its arm and ribs hanging free from its main torso. Two Catchers were with Zandibar and fighting hard; the distance shortened. Too many creatures slowed their path and the fighting was fierce. Soon ogres and orcs were everywhere and Slassiantha was fighting alongside Kerstan and Morning Dew. Other Zinobian warriors appeared, killing foe effortlessly to help in the fight. Although outclassed by the Zinobians, the creatures still took casualties due to their mass. Zinobian warriors lay dead or injured but still they fought bravely.

The battlements of the city finally could take no more and split, hanging wildly in the wind from the splintered frame. Hundreds of creatures pushed forwards in frenzy. Orders were screamed from orc leaders and the battle took on another level.

"Take the city, burn, and kill them all. Let no one live," yelled one of the orc leaders, his cruel, ugly face screwed up in triumph as he yelled. "Destroy the Source, destroy them all!"

Chaos took control of the city men and many turned to retreat further into the city itself. Orcs rushed in and soon fires were started and buildings were pulled down; all in the path died: man, women or child – none were spared. Theorn desperately tried to regain control before he too was forced to retreat deeper into the city. The few Sleepers still alive, having lost their influence and control from Snode, were running wild, eating and killing all around them. Drawn by magic, they headed slowly towards the chapel and the Source.

In the chapel the Source was decaying badly. The strain on her resources was too great, yet she had to continue. The Zenithe suffered under her demands for power, but obediently continued to serve. Large chunks of honeycomb lay loosely on the floor unattended due to other demands. News of the battlements having given way filtered into the chapel and the Zenithe began to defend the chapel as well as the Source.

Zandibar rose in a slow, cumbersome fashion, weary and hurt from his exertion, and surveyed the battle around him. Only a short distance away and moving towards him at a slow pace was Kerstan. Kerstan slashed this way and that, carving a path through the creatures, his speed and skill allowing few attacks to penetrate his defence. One glancing blow had clipped him across the cheek and a trickle of fresh blood ran down mingled with his sweat. Rubbing the cut occasionally with his forearm Kerstan fought on, closing the distance between him and Zandibar. Slassiantha was close by and defended Kerstan as she made her way closer. She seemed to glide this way and that, avoiding most attacks with ease. Morning Dew was creating a big impression in the mass of creatures. Untiring, she had cut, stabbed and smashed trolls and orcs aside with increasing speed, her small muscular body moving at such a pace that the creatures were unable to make any decent attack and had to defend instead. Zandibar began fighting once again with Strika (the other Catcher) defending his tiring body. His body, although old, was not slow, and with some ease he moved among the orcs and other creatures, causing problems. Kerstan, nearing Zandibar, bent down and hooked the Catcher up, flipping him onto his back. With Zandibar holding on tightly, Kerstan began making his way towards the city.

"Hold tight. We need to get to the Source."

Kerstan's voice was laboured and forced, and sweat was pouring off him as he pushed on. The battle's fierceness had taken its toll on him and he was struggling now. As Kerstan had bent to hook Zandibar a troll had swung a club that changed direction at the last second and smashed harmlessly into a rock nearby. Slassiatha lowered her arm and wearily smiled as she pushed herself to stay close to Kerstan. Slassiantha was feeling drawn and needed to rest but pushed on anyway. Slicing hard the troll fell under her blade. Zandibar closed his eyes and a low glow surrounded Kerstan then drifted to Slassiantha. Instantly both felt the power flow over them: muscles ached no more and energy filled their bodies. Feeling a little more refreshed they battled on with a new fervour towards the city and the devastation now within its walls.

Morning Dew was as fresh as when she had first dismounted her Roc, and accurately killed all that stood in her path. Her Roc helped to keep a wide area around her as it bobbed in and out, lifting and then dropping creatures dead or injured. Distinctively, the Roc seemed to know her mistress's moves and was able to protect her from most attacks. Zinobians were fighting hard everywhere with other Rocs, working their skill in much the same way.

Shadma, using his size and weight continually, kept beating the orcs back; Buckenbear was close. Although both tired they were fighting hard.

Greatbird was moving in a smooth fashion, well rehearsed in battle. Her great axe whirled in every direction, accurately slaying its intended. Somersaulting one orc, she imbedded the blade deeply and, using the orc as a lever, flew high over two others. The blade flashed and both fell; upon landing the blade finished its course, embedding in a troll and crunching its skull in two. So far her task of keeping Morning Dew in view was accomplished.

Theorn gathered some city folk together and charged the oncoming orcs. He had to delay the attack somehow, so with desperation he threw himself into the task ahead of him. Taken by surprise, the orcs backed off a little only to turn and return back into the fight. Regrouping, Theorn attempted another attack, and soon others joined the attack. The city folk were holding their own but for how long? Several Rocs suddenly flew over low, grabbing orcs as they passed, with the Zinobians slicing at others as they flew past. Soon the Zinobian warriors were fighting hard also. Through the broken gates and over the battlements poured hordes of creatures. The rain had slowed slightly and looked as if it may slow or even stop. The clouds were not so dark and the red tinge had left them. Soon the city folk were heavily outnumbered. The great mass of creatures slowly destroyed their way towards the chapel.

Greatbird dived and rolled, seemly untouchable; orcs fell left and right. Suddenly a huge ogre stood before her and swinging its heavy mace hard just clipped her ankle. Knocked to the ground, Greatbird rolled and although severe pain now held her, regained her feet, finishing the Ogre easily, its body falling heavily as its head left its shoulders.

Through the mass of creatures a strange wild-cat-like creature pounced, its sharp claws outstretched to kill. Only Greatbird's skill allowed her to roll to safety. The Sleeper swung its whip hard, wrapping the long evil rope around Greatbird's axe. Pulling hard, the axe moved but under the strong grip of Greatbird stayed safely in her hand. The Sleeper stood erect and shot a fear glare attack at her, and even as fearless as Greatbird was it unnerved her, and Greatbird took a defensive stance. The Sleeper circled and made to pounce again. Greatbird tensed and readied herself. Suddenly a massive fiery Roc appeared and stood in the middle of the two; its eyes shone angrily. The Sleeper pounced and the Roc avoided the attack and counterattacked, missing by a fraction the hind flank of the Sleeper. Soon Sleeper and Roc were circling and trying to outmanoeuvre each other. Greatbird stood still and watched for other attackers unable to join the fight, waiting for the chance and defending in the meantime. The Sleepers senses were raging, magic was everywhere around this creature; adrenalin pumping hard in its veins, it continued to attack. Each attack was countered then an attack was made. After a short time the Sleeper saw its opening and plunged its teeth deep into the body of the Roc. Teeth crunching hard on nothing made the Sleeper shut its eyes in pain. Greatbird took her chance and her axe hit the Sleeper hard on the upward motion, directly under its protective armour-like top. The blow sent the body physically up into the air, splitting in two as it flew. Upon landing the front half made a last attempt to attack, faltered, then died.

Morning Dew staggered weakened by the image; Slassiantha was quick to react and helped her keep her feet while slicing away at an orc that attacked. Kerstan was there helping also. Greatbird took one last look at the Sleeper then smiled across at Morning Dew before lunging hard back into the fray. Kerstan started back towards the battlements with Zandibar on his back; Slassiantha stayed back to help give Morning Dew the time needed to recover. The other Catcher went with Kerstan to help. Slassiantha fought hard, using her skill and magic to delay the attack upon them both. Whistling loudly, Slassiantha continued to fight and motioned to the sky. Quickly from the sky came Morning Dew's Roc. It slammed hard into the orcs and goblins, scattering them then taking flight once again before landing. The gap needed to be big enough to land and long enough to have Morning Dew in her talons, held with a loving grip. Greatbird joined Slassiantha in beating back the mass of creatures, unsure of what to do – Morning Dew was in need of rest but rest was weak and Zinobians showed no weakness. After a while other Zinobians joined in the attempt. Slowly the gap appeared and once the gap appeared so did the Roc. Up she flew and out of danger, flying hard away back towards her camp and safety.

Slassiantha, as soon as the Roc left, was in pursuit of Kerstan, Greatbird and the others giving her the help she needed. Greatbird felt mixed emotions: glad to see her daughter safe yet it was weak. The battle soon stopped, Greatbird thinking too deeply about her problem, and then the fight went on.

Morning Dew, slowly clearing her vision, fought to turn the Roc back towards the battle. The Roc turned and flew back obediently as Morning Dew climbed back on her back. Once up, Morning Dew took several deep breaths and held on, trying not to fall or pass out. Only her determination held her in the saddle.

Slassiantha fought hard and fast, making her way towards Kerstan and Zandibar. Kerstan was a good distance away and could be seen fighting hard, making progress in getting to the battlements. Zandibar and the other Catcher were beside him, fighting hard also. Inside the city walls the creatures were deep in the city and closing in on the chapel. Orcs, goblins and other creatures massed the outer city, having forced the folk defending deeper into the centre of the city itself and closer to the chapel. Theorn was fronting attack after attack with some success, yet the creatures moved forward.

Outside the battlements the battle raged on also. Shadma and the other giants were making a small difference, using their size and skills to their advantage. Zinobian warriors massed here and there, causing a great amount of damage. Alanthos and Buckenbear were still close together and several horsemen had joined them. The weather was calming but left the ground a sticky mass of boggy material, slowing all who walked its paths. Heavily outnumbered, the city folk and other defenders were showing signs of despair and fatigue.

Flying low over the battle came the Rocs carrying Zinobians and the Catchers. Several orcs fell as they passed. Flying deep into the grounds, they dropped near the chapel to allow the Catchers to dismount and some of the Zinobians joined them. Upon dismounting, all were instantly in a major battle and fought hard in the attempt to gain access to the chapel grounds. As they neared the grounds, from within the border fences that separated the battle and the chapel grounds came several of the Zenithe. Clothed in white and moving swiftly, they came with flashes of yellow light, creating an opening in the mass of creatures. Fighting hard, the Zinobians made space for the Catchers to move to the gates and through. The gates shut quickly behind them and the Zinobians defended along with the city folk; to allow the Catchers time to leave for the chapel three Zinobians were going with them. The gates and surrounding fences would not hold long and the creatures kept coming.

Ushering the Catchers into the chapel, the great entrance doors were re-closed and a massive beam placed to prevent entry. It only took a short while before the creatures forced entrance into the grounds and the battle continued hard in there also.

Kerstan swung his sword hard, knocking two orcs aside and pushed on the gates in sight. Zandibar and Strika were close behind; their burgundy bodies moved fast and smoothly in and out of trouble and headed slowly towards the gates also. The only time they slowed or stopped was to defend or attack all who opposed them. Slassiantha had gained ground and with her were Greatbird and her guards.

113

All around the battle raged, the weather improving the ground upon which they fought. Dead lay wherever the eyes looked and injured were left to die as the battle continued. Although progress was slow, Slassiatha and Greatbird had closed the gap between themselves and Kerstan. From a distance, screaming like a banshee and thrashing madly and uncontrollably with his sword, came Mutley, sweat pouring from his body but with a triumphant grin upon his face.

With the gate in sight they pushed hard. Slowly Kerstan, Zandibar and Strika made their way towards the gates that hung precariously from their hinges. Greatbird and Slassiantha were close behind causing damage as well.

The Source lay heavily upon the bark of the oak, its skin in disarray with large gaping holes that hung here and there. Light was fading from the honeycomb shape. The Catchers and Zenithe fought hard to preserve the material, power leaving their bodies in great amounts. Several Catchers stood together; spikes raised and with front legs raised, they closed their eyes. Concentrating, they threw all the power they possessed at the Source. A bright burgundy glow covered the Source. Small areas began to move and repair them. The Source took in their magic and began utilising the uses it had, although the process was slow. Outside the chapel the results took place slowly; people took on new vigour, pushing the enemy back slowly. Injured began to heal and broken limbs repair. The giants with their new found strength began bashing great numbers aside and moving to help others around them. Encouraged, the city folk pushed on harder. The creatures were slowly being pushed back.

Inside the chapel the Catchers were worried: the magic was not catching and was draining as fast as it was given. While they gave the Source was helped; if they stopped then the Source began to waver. The Source was dying and their power was limited. Where was Zandibar? He would have the knowledge of what to do; he had been there when his parents created the Source. The Zenithe had given all they could and needed to rest; the Catchers, although much more powerful, could not continue indefinitely. How long had the Source kept its need quiet? Was their effort too late and why had She not told sooner?

With sheer determination and a sense of duty, they battled on. Kerstan had travelled a great distance and through many troubles to get their help and they had to do their best. Was their best good enough though?

Zandibar and Kerstan weaved towards the gates as quickly as they could. Both tired, they pushed themselves to continue. Only determination moved them on; Zandibar used all his skill and speed to outwit the enemy and Kerstan used his power to back him up. Kerstan was a powerful man and highly skilled, and smashed several aside, preventing them from slowing their progress. It seemed every creature imaginable stood in their path: goblin, orc, troll and ogre, yet still they moved on. Zinobians were near, helping to level the sides as they killed in great numbers and with speed. Slassiantha, Greatbird, and Strika were near and helped also.

Morning Dew was feeling better and steered her Roc to help also. Flying low, she attacked all the Roc flew over. Suddenly the Roc veered sharply and only skill held Morning Dew on its strong back. The blow had come quick and unexpected; a troll hit hard with its club, hitting the wing a violent blow that jerked the Roc sideways. As it righted itself the second blow came, this one hitting it under the wing on its belly. Rearing hard, the Roc screeched loudly as it rose violently into the air, throwing Morning Dew off in an awkward angle. Hitting the floor hard, the wind left her lungs; with fire in her throat Morning Dew rolled and stumbled to her feet, only to collapse as quickly in severe pain – no weight could be put on the leg. Nausea passed over her and the world started to black out, but Morning Dew determinedly crawled back to her knees.

The orcs were upon her as soon as she hit the ground, only her speed and skill held their blades from harming her. Suddenly the orcs scattered as her Roc swept in low and tried to hook her up in its claws. The orcs were back and forced the Roc to take flight again. Strika and Greatbird joined in, attempting to clear the room around Morning Dew. The Roc flew in again, scattering the creatures once again. Morning Dew, knowing that she was going to hinder the rest, took her sword and raising it high plunged it towards her own stomach. As the blade drew near an axe knocked it aside; Greatbird looked harshly at her then turned the blade, killing another orc that got too near. As the gap opened her Roc plunged, gripping her protesting into the air. Immense pain rushed through her leg and Morning Dew passed out. The bird flew up and up out of danger, then turned to fly once again back to camp.

Slowly Kerstan and Zandibar had moved forward with the Source's help and now they entered the city gates. The giants, with their strength returning, had pushed closer to the walls; creatures flew in all directions under each blow. Zinobian warriors, their beautiful bodies moving in a graceful fashion out of place in such an awful battle, were everywhere, killing and maiming as they went. Although taking losses they were killing more than losing. Their Rocs flew in and out in quick repetitive movements, complementing their owners each time they did. Slowly the city looked as if possibly it may be defended after all. Many had died, many were injured, yet pride held each strong and close. Buckenbear was still fighting hard and enjoying the thrill and challenge: his face held a look of total ecstasy as he thrashed about. Maxinton had joined Shadma and both had formed an almost unbeatable technique of fighting.

Kerstan slashed hard and wildly as they pushed their way through the gates. Looking around revealed total devastation: buildings in ruin, on fire or partially burnt. Cattle were loose and roaming the battle ground, trampling dead or injured as they avoided the crazed creatures that remained around them. Women and children were amongst the dead and the whole area was one of destruction. The main thing Kerstan noticed was the lack of creatures and folk about still standing. All had moved deeper into the city and were drawing ever closer to the chapel and the Source. Fighting the few left they made their way deeper into the city. They had to be on time, they had to be!

It was not long after that Slassiantha, Greatbird and Strika were at the gates. However, the creatures outside were fighting back and the defences were failing so they stayed at the gates and helped hold back the creatures, their pursuit of Zandibar and Kerstan put to one side. It was more important to delay further entrance than to join them, so they fought hard and fast.


The young Roc had flown hard and fast until out of immediate danger, then had settled into a steady pace. Clutched carefully in its claws hung the limp body of its friend and mistress, Morning Dew. Tiring from its injury, the Roc slowly settled the limp frame to the ground before settling down next to it to rest. Breathing heavily, the Roc lowered its head and drank from a small stream nearby. The landing had shaken Morning Dew and caused her to moan as she regained consciousness. Her leg burned fiercely, the pain making her want to be sick. Swallowing hard, she forced herself upright and felt a wave of dizziness wash over herself. Slowly she sat herself up, breathing heavily and fast so as not to pass out again. Examining her leg, she found that the shape was twisted and the leg itself was badly swollen. Cross that she had lost her weapon and confused at her mother's actions, she sat rubbing the leg.

Considering her next move she sat looking around the area which was quiet and free from life yet full of destruction. Trees were split and broken, bushes torn up or damaged, and some distance away lay a body being picked at by vultures as they squabbled over the find. Culturally, she should take her own life; she was going to slow the tribe and may never fully recover the use of her damaged limb. Yet her mother, the Chief, had spared her life by knocking aside the blade! All this was not easy to comprehend.

Her thoughts were broken by a nudge from behind. The Roc had approached and gently nudged her with its beak. Idly, she stroked the Roc's neck absent-mindedly. Morning Dew made to stand but the pain caused her to sit again. Feeling sick and angry, she punched the ground. The young Roc nudged her again and pushed its strong neck under her arm, raising it gently. The Roc snorted a low gentle snort from its nose and waited. Morning Dew put out her arm and grabbed the feathers behind the neck hard in a vice grip. As the Roc slowly lifted her body the pain returned, causing Morning Dew to wince and take a sharp intake of breath. The Roc reacted and twisting its strong neck, placed her body gently on its back. Wincing with pain, Morning Dew held tightly until the sickness passed then, kicking with her good leg, she guided the Roc up into the air again. Once up in the air the Roc took flight back towards camp, but Morning Dew had to see her mother again. Slowly she indicated to the Roc that she wished to return to the battle. The Roc went to resist but responded to the action and, turning slowly, flew back the way it had come.


Kerstan and Zandibar moved as safely and quickly as they could. They travelled for a few minutes before seeing the large group of creatures circling the fences and trying to enter the grounds of the chapel. The battle was at its peak and all the city folk were fighting hard to stop the advance of the creatures. The way ahead blocked, they had to see if there was an alternative route they could take as the Source needed their assistance as quickly as they could get to it. Back at the main gates the creatures had penetrated the defences again and were beginning to pour in through the gaps in the defences. Slassiantha and Greatbird were fighting hard alongside the other Zinobians and city folk. However hard they all fought, the mass of creatures was just too big and slowly advanced.

Inside the inner chamber of the chapel there was a hive of activity.

Catchers moved here and there, mending and re-mending small breaks and large gaping holes that appeared in the honeycomb frame. The Zenithe had begun to accompany them in the task and the results were looking reasonable yet seemed not to last. The honeycomb shone a low burgundy glow and shook gently under the magic. Some of the Zenithe had left the chamber in the attempt to slow the creatures, joining the city folk in the defences. The occasional bolt of yellow energy sent creatures into a deep sleep: where they were cut down where they stood.

Kerstan and Zandibar moved as quickly and as quietly as they could, using all the stealth they could muster. Taking a wide birth of the creatures, they made their way around the perimeter of the chapel buildings. After a few minutes they found that towards the back of the building there were not too many creatures as the walls were high and there was no entrance other than a small window high up on the wall. The walls were carefully made and would be virtually impossible to climb. Moving quickly, Kerstan killed the two orcs near them then moved on to the last four that noticed them. Once they were dead he took from his backpack a rope and a grappling hook. Slowly and deliberately he began swinging the hook around his head, widening the arc and building up the speed. As he did, Zandibar attempted climbing the wall only to fall after a few feet. Releasing the rope, the hook flew fast and accurately at the window but fell short by several feet. Gathering up the rope again he began to swing again, while watching for any creatures that may have seen them. Zandibar began watching for their advancement to give the time needed.

Every movement made by the Roc shot pain through Morning Dew's leg yet she continued to guide the bird slowly back. Flying high over the battle, she watched the mass of creatures below as they fought the city folk. All the time she scanned the ground for any sign of her mother or Slassiantha. She had passed over three times and had not seen them among the mass of movement, not wanting to fly too low. Morning Dew could see two different battles going on: one at the walls where the mass of creatures slowly moved forwards into the city grounds, the other deeper in the city towards the centre where there was a chapel that seemed to be under siege. Where were they? She had circled several times and not seen any of them. Taking the Roc lower slightly, she circled once more. As the bird moved lower, Morning Dew saw Zandibar then she saw Kerstan. Turning the Roc she pushed it to fly even lower so that she could see what they were doing. As she flew lower several creatures noticed and started making their way around to confront her. Once lower Morning Dew could see what Kerstan was attempting to do. Kerstan had stopped upon hearing the Roc approach; drawing his sword he looked urgently at the Roc and rider.

Morning Dew had to act fast and pushed the Roc to land a little hard. The Roc hit the floor, stumbled, then righted itself. Pain shot up Morning Dew's leg; nausea followed as quickly. Fighting the feeling, Morning Dew grabbed at Zandibar who upon realising who the rider was obliged in jumping on the back of the Roc. As Kerstan joined Zandibar several orcs turned the corner. Soon the air was full of arrows that flew in rapid succession at the Roc and its occupants. Kicking hard with her good leg, Morning Dew tried to encourage the Roc to take flight again. The Roc bucked and reared, trying to avoid the arrows and fly away. As the Roc flew, several arrows whizzed past narrowly missing, one hitting the underside of the Roc and one hitting Kerstan in the arm. All held on to the crazed creature as it fought to stay in control. Kerstan, gritting his teeth, tore the arrow free then tossed it to the ever-decreasing ground below. The Roc was now rising awkwardly out of arrow reach; its breathing was hard and fast. The arrow lodged in her lung she flew on. Several more arrows flew past, narrowly missing before they were far enough away.

Kerstan pointed to the window and Morning Dew made to guide the Roc closer. More arrows came at them and the Roc bucked hard to avoid them. Morning Dew lost her grip and slipped awkwardly from the Roc's back. Kerstan was seated just behind Morning Dew and grabbed at her and caught her by her leather armour. Morning Dew hung precariously in the air for several seconds until Kerstan help her back onto the tiring Roc. The Roc took flight and rose higher, fearing for its life. Several seconds passed before Kerstan managed to get control again, then Morning Dew guided the Roc to circle the wall of the chapel.

To the other side of the tower was a small area where someone could stand to observe the area. No more than possibly two people could stand on the area at a time. Next to the area was a door of wood that was tightly shut. This was their only chance now as the creatures were below were in big numbers. Morning Dew took the neck of the Roc and gently spoke to it as she guided it slowly towards the small area. The Roc was now breathing in a spasmodic fashion and was very laboured. Once near, Morning Dew tried to hold the Roc steady as Zandibar and Kerstan tried to jump to the ground. Just as they prepared to jump, the Roc lost height and brushed against the wall. Bucking hard, the Roc tried to right itself then flew on with Morning Dew barely holding on. Upon contact, Kerstan and Zandibar had been thrown from the Roc. Landing heavily, they both managed to hold onto the area. Kerstan hung to the wall before pulling himself up. Zanibar had jumped quicker and had landed on the ground safely.

Once on the ground both turned to see the Roc and Morning Dew flying awkwardly away with Morning Dew holding on precariously with the Roc's troubled flight. Soon they both were out of view behind some trees. Kerstan turned to the door and tried it; the door held fast and was locked. Looking around Kerstan took two small steps backwards to the edge of the area. Placing his feet carefully he looked over the edge: far below the creatures fought hard trying to gain entry into the chapel. Kerstan looked once again towards the door then ran hard and fast against the door with his good shoulder. Pain shot up his arm where the arrow had shot and the door held. With his whole body jarred, Kerstan hit the floor. Quickly he stood and stepped back to attempt another charge at the door. This time he put everything he had into the charge. Upon hitting the door a cracking sound came from the doorframe. Looking Kerstan saw that the door had moved and the frame was splitting. Inside noise could be heard of someone coming. Quickly he tried again and the door gave way enough to look in upon two tall white figures with a yellow haze about them.

As the door went the Zenithe were ready, with their arms up they prepared to defend the tower. The door sprang open and there stood Kerstan sword in hand and a small burgundy Catcher. Slowly the glow left their hands and the Zenithe ushered them inside. Once inside the sound of battle was loud and the Zenithe signalled to move fast and quietly after them. Quickly they travelled over the Zenithe and city folk that fought hard below, oblivious to the passing people above. They travelled down a small staircase and then turned into a corridor with a door at the end. Once at the door the Zenithe, using magic, opened the door and ushered them through, then the door shut tight behind and resealed itself. Onward they went to another door that the Zenithe opened also, once inside several anxious Zenithes and Catchers were working hard to look after a sorry looking Source which faced Kerstan and Zandibar. Power was everywhere and the hair on Kerstan stood up instantly. Several Zenithe that had blocked their entrance, upon seeing them, had stepped aside.

The Roc had flown as far as it could, its breathing had become laboured and its energy had diminished so badly that it had had to land. Only a few hundred feet from the chapel the Roc lay exhausted and dying. Morning Dew had thrown herself clear from the Roc and lay in agony nearby. Aware of danger everywhere, the young Roc forced itself up and slowly placed its wing gently over Morning Dew to protect, then its head sagged and the Roc died. Morning Dew, exhausted and in considerable pain, could not find the strength to move the wing and collapsed asleep in the field.

Slassiantha and Greatbird continued to fight hard, defending each other as they did. Several other Zinobian warriors were with them and the progress was good. With the city folk helping, they had slowed and virtually stopped the creatures from entering the main city. The giants were at the back of the mass of fighting. Shadma and Maxinton led the attacks and were causing damage to the ranks. So far the Source had held and the magic had stopped the creatures. So far the city stood, but for how long?

Zandibar walked slowly into the room; upon seeing the Source so ill he had felt sick. Shaking with grief and rage the Catcher moved towards the sorry honeycomb frame. Several Catchers stood aside in anticipation. Zandibar's thoughts went to his parents. They had helped in the creation of the Source and then they had died due to the Source and its weakness to see the greed of the humans. He had been there and seen the miracle and now he stood upon the same creation dying in front of him. Decay held the Source and large patches were open and damaged even though the Catchers and Zenithe still poured magic into its mighty frame. The great oak that held it seemed to sense the loss and drooped slightly in the knowledge that something was not right. The Catchers had come to help but even with their magic the Source was dying. Why had his kind allowed this to happen? Zandibar looked around the room, his emotions in tatters. Why had the Source kept quiet for so long and why had the Source allowed the humans to do this to itself? Anger and confusion ran through the Catcher's mind. Zandibar stood still and watched in desperation, what could he do to help? Kerstan was close by, unable to take in the difference in the Source and feeling sick to the core. Were they too late?

Zandibar moved slowly closer to the Source and raised his hand; his intention was to touch the hurting Source and comfort. However to touch the Source was forbidden and could be dangerous, so the Zenithe stood in the way of Zandibar. That is how it had started, with humans touching the frame and draining the Source. Zandibar moved aside and then once past the Zenith touched the sorry frame gently; full of compassion he poured power into the Source and stood there crying.

"I'm so sorry for letting this happen."

Zanzibar's thoughts had rushed from him like a torrent and the Source glowed brightly as it replied.

"NO! I am the one who is sorry! It was I who failed you, not anyone else!"

Zandibar was visibly shaken yet continued to touch the Source.

Zandibar straightened himself then took a deep breath, physically corrected his posture then spoke again. "No, that is not right. I will not fail you again."

As soon as the words left his mind Zandibar threw his whole body hard into the honeycomb frame. Instantly the frame shook and glowed with a magnificent brightness. Kerstan was there but was stopped by the Zenithe, unable to do anything but watch helplessly he gaped upon the whole incident. Zandibar squirmed then opened his mouth to scream, his face contorted but nothing came out. The Source became brighter and began to repair itself, all around stopped what they were doing and just watched. Slowly Zandibar's face turned to a broad grin, then his body began to shake and break up, dissolving into the Source. All his love and forgiveness poured into the Source. Zandibar seemed to be laughing and the Source responded by glowing brighter. More and more patches repaired and the gaping holes disappeared. All around the room the Zenithe were being refreshed and healed, the Catchers the same. Kerstan felt pure love pour over his body and the wounds gathered in battle disappear. Kerstan just stared at the sacrifice made by Zandibar and shook his head in disbelief.

At the city wall the creatures were fighting hard; they began to force back the city folk and Slassiantha and Greatbird tried to regroup the men quickly. Suddenly there was a blinding bright light, golden in colour, that swept over the ground in mighty waves, coming from within the city itself. All around the ground shook and opened up, swallowing the creatures and miraculously ignoring the city folk, Zinobians and all who defended the city. Orcs, goblins and trolls fell into the holes; everywhere utter chaos broke out. All over the place people were being healed or refreshed. Each rush of light touched more and more, and soon all the attacking creatures were gone and the entire city folk and helpers were healed or refreshed. All but the dead: they had been swallowed with the creatures.

Slassiantha looked on in wonder, Greatbird by her side, both shocked yet happy. After a short time cheers began to sound as people realised the connection. The Source was well again, the city was safe once again. Looking around Slassiantha saw Alanthos coming at speed in the distance, his muscular body fit and well, his arms held out ready to hold her tightly. Soon he reached her and lifted her body free from the ground, hugging her tightly. As he did both cried freely. Greatbird stood among her warriors: a proud leader, her eyes scanning the area. Uncertain thoughts crossed her mind. Had she led her warriors into a battle that was right, had she lost too many, was Morning Dew alive or had she accomplished killing herself?

City folk were spilling from the city walls, celebrating with all they met. Soon a great celebration was happening. With the folk were Kerstan and the Catchers and, much to Greatbird's delight, Morning Dew. Morning Dew, upon seeing her mum, ran to greet her; her leg had suddenly healed when the ground shook around her. Nearing, she slowed then stopped a few feet away, unsure of her mum's reaction. Greatbird walked over slowly and as she did Morning Dew held herself tall and proudly. Greatbird, upon reaching Morning Dew, brushed her up in her strong bronzed arms and hugged her, unashamed that she loved her daughter. Both laughed and pushed apart, taking on the form of great warriors once again.

It took several months for the land around to turn green again. The city was rebuilt and the neighbouring villages repaired. Some progress was made between the giants and humans. Even the odd giant was accepted in the city and not frowned upon. Buckenbear and all the mercenaries who had survived were paid and left, back to their own private lives. With the Source better soon all were well and crops began to grow. Treaties were formed and life began to correct itself once again. Greatbird and Morning Dew, after some consideration, left the Zinobian tribe and as a form of gratitude for their efforts were bought a small farm near the city. As time went on the war was forgotten. Stories were told and retold till the stories became legends, and legends may or may not be real.


The wagon bobbed gently as the traveller spoke to his son. The sun shone brightly and the day was drawing in. The man in his mid twenties smiled to his son. Young at eight yet even at such an age willing and able to learn the trade of a traveller. The city of Greatoak in was sight, its magnificent walls shining in the evening sun. It was to be their last port of call before nightfall, then they would return home back to his wife and relax for a while.

The road narrowed a little as the hills rolled close to the roadside. Slowing the horse, Johan looked about easily. All seemed well so on he went. Just as they passed the hills the bandits attacked. They came quickly, their horses riding hard over the hills. Johan died before he could draw his own bow. The horse and cart was eventually stopped and then taken. No one had noticed the little boy who had jumped from the cart and hidden amongst the rocks.

Drako sat still and waited long after the bandits had gone, frightened to move. As the sun settled he decided to make his move for the city and its safety. Getting up he moved from the safety of the rocks. No one about. He moved in the direction of the city. It was then that he saw the staff. It was an odd looking thing. It looked like an old withered branch with a brier wrapped tightly around it. Slowly he approached it then bent to pick it up. Holding the branch in his hand he felt great power humming from within it. Drako held it up and took a closer look, as he did the brier loosened and moved quickly around the young boy's arm. Soon the spikes were embedded deep in his arm. Drako tried to drop the branch but his arm would not respond. Power poured into his body, images of violence and destruction followed. He saw two grotesque creatures die and felt like they were his parents. Anger rose in his head and the power fed on the anger. More images poured into his vulnerable mind. Soon Drako believed that he was someone called Snode and he was the most powerful creature alive. Images of tall black mountains crossed his mind, then of a cave and of three men within the cave. Then the voice spoke to him. The voice was an evil and controlling voice.

"Go to the Tomb of the Tainted, gather help and destroy the Source."

An evil grin crossed the young face and then he began to laugh

an evil laugh. This time he would make certain he was ready, then when he was older and really ready he would destroy the city and avenge his parents.

Years passed and all of Greatoak lived in harmony; the Source provided so that they lived in some comfort. Over the years the stories changed, some got exaggerated, some were totally made up. It was years since the great battle and had it really happened or was it just a story told to please or scare all who listened? As the city folk enjoyed their lives, on a hill that looked upon the city stood a young man in his mid-twenties. He wore a dark robe and carried an odd looking staff. It looked like a branch with a brier tightly bound around it. The man stood there and just grinned to himself, a sly and evil grin.